The
PROMISE

Book One of The Shepherd Chronicles

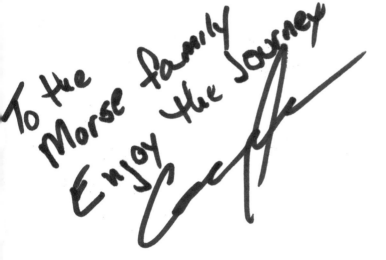

GARY FRIEDMAN

ISBN: 978-1-4834-4739-1 (sc)
ISBN: 978-1-4834-4738-4 (e)

Lulu Publishing Services rev. date: 03/03/2016

Contents

Dedication

NOT ALL THINGS HAVE JUST one birth date. David as the Flockless Shepherd was first born into my subconscious on Thanksgiving morning in 2005. Except for a few written words and an outline, he remained there for more than six years.

It wasn't until the early spring of 2012 that he was reborn through the encouragement and support of one very special person. I know the term *muse* is overused in the world today. But in this case it could not be a truer description. Just as David changed lives forever, this woman changed mine.

Thank you Denise, not only for myself, but for the flock yet to be defined. You are my muse, my best friend. Yours until...

Acknowledgements

No one starts a project such as this at any point in their life without the guidance and support of many people.

I tapped several people for their expertise on subject matter. Dr. Lori Michael assisted with medical issues and was very supportive of the project. Her expertise in emergency rooms and with trauma pointed me in the right direction. Ron Adimey knows the bar business as well as anyone on Earth and allowed me to pick his brain to create clubs as locations. Kevin Babcock, firearms instructor, kept me on target with the weapons used in this story.

I was blessed with the help of two women who assisted with editing as the project picked up speed. Judy O'Brien and Darcy Thiel both donated their time and expertise to make me sound smart.

I am also blessed to have four wonderful children, Leslie, Isabel, Ethan and Leah, who have stood by my side throughout my journey, as well as the writing of this book. They have always been my inspiration.

I would also like to thank Tyson Roberts and his team at Lulu Publishing for believing in me and taking my dream to heart.

And finally, this book never would have advanced beyond a dream state without the encouragement, belief, support, initial editing and love of Denise O'Brien.

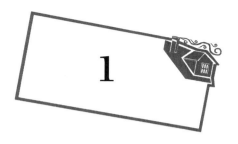

1

The Promise

*I*T BEGINS WITH A VAGUE *buzzing sound and a dim glow. It's as if I am an old-time radio and my tubes are just getting some juice. This is the first hint that I'm still among the living. At least I think I am. I can feel the presence of others around me, but I can't communicate. My eyes are closed, my body motionless. The last thing I can recall is driving along the I-290 deep in thought, forgetting the surprises that the roads in Buffalo can offer in the dead of winter.*

I hear voices. Some I know, some I don't recognize. "Mom…what's wrong? Why are you crying? What do you mean it's all your fault?"

Nope, don't know that voice. Kind of cold, serious, businesslike – but whoever it is, he knows my name. David.

Oh, that buzzing sound again, drowning out the voices. How did I get here? I remember the wedding and my parents being there and being frustrated by feelings I had buried for so very long. I recall loading up the car, expecting the roads to be more snow-covered than they appeared to be.

The voices again. It's Dad. We talked for so long tonight. It is still tonight, isn't it? I feel the same anger at him that I had felt while we talked. It came back so quickly. Where is the closeness we used to share, the closeness I'd been missing, the closeness I remember while growing up?

No pain, none at all. Is that good or bad? Is this how dying feels? So many questions. I feel disconnected, like I'm floating above it all.

"Mom, I want to come home, start over. There is so much to live for." I was thinking that when…damn…when was that?

This isn't one of those I'm-too-young-to-die things. It's more like, I'm just not done yet. I was put here for a purpose I haven't fulfilled. Dad used to remind me about that all the time. "God's path," he called it. He said I had been on that path, but I fell off. And not just a step off into some bushes, more like falling off a cliff. I remember seeing that path again while we talked at the wedding, the way I used to. Not as clearly, of course. Not without the bitterness between us, but still real.

There was a field behind our house when I was a kid, with a path through it to the Brighton Pool. I can see that field now, and the huge oak tree that towered nearby.

I remember so clearly now. Twenty years ago, at the age of five, I almost fell out of that oak tree. I had to hang on until my friend Doug could pull me back to a safe branch. That was the first time I begged God for help. "Save me God, save me. Please don't let me fall. I promise I'll be good. I promise I'll listen to Mom and Dad. I promise, God, just don't let me die."

I can also remember the day they cut that tree down. It had been my protector. God had reached His hand out to me for the first time there, in that tree, and then it was gone. Just to put in that stupid road.

That tree was right near Colvin Boulevard… wait…Colvin? I remember seeing that street sign tonight. But it wasn't going by my side window like it was supposed to. Instead, it was moving across my windshield. I was careening sideways, right where my tree used to be.

Twenty years later and I'm back at the same spot, near my tree, with the same plea. "Save me, God. Don't let me fall. Don't let me die." I remember that relationship I had once with God. He made that path for me, cut it out with His own hands. He not only saved me in that field, He was my oak tree. "Don't let me fall, God. I just found Dad again. Mom needs me. Jeannie and Hannah can't grow up without their big brother. I still have so much to accomplish, so many songs to write, to sing."

The vision of that Colvin Boulevard sign comes back, sliding across my windshield – where it shouldn't be. And those headlights shouldn't be coming closer, growing bigger. And I beg God for help for the second time in my life. "Oh, God, don't let me fall. I promise I'll be good!"

Darkness. Cold darkness. And the buzzing doesn't go away. Come on, eyes, open...let me see my family...let me just move a toe…pull me back, Dougie…I have to get through this…

"God, please don't take me now. I haven't finished Your work yet. I know You put me here to follow a path, but I failed. Please Father, give me a chance to redeem myself. I promise I will live my life to serve You. I promise."

The buzzing fades. I'm almost at peace. No pain. No voices. Like a deep sleep. Just a single tear rolling down my cheek and onto the pillow.

One patch of ice, and I found it. One truck on the road, and it found me. All where an oak tree used to stand, the spot where I first found God. The same spot where He found me, again.

What are the odds?

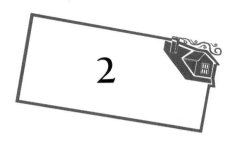

The Dreamer

I REALLY EXPECTED MUCH BETTER service from a $140 pair of running shoes. The left one has stalled on the first wooden step of the deck. I suppose it isn't the shoe's fault; my whole body is frozen. The last place I expected to find myself, after leaving Buffalo for Nashville over a year ago, was looking up at this familiar sight. The Breakwall is the flagship location of the best chain of clubs in all of Western New York. This Lake Erie beach resort would surprise any out-of-towner who visits Buffalo expecting only drifts of snow and screeching, frigid winds. And this club would hold its own against clubs in more traditional beach resort towns. It is the pride and joy of Jacob Horlansky.

It wasn't that long ago that I was the up-and-coming superstar in Jacob's favorite playground. We had met at a private function where I was working as a bartender. Jacob was a guest, but as a man who loves the bar business, whoever served the drinks was his best friend. I was never shy behind a bar, but Jacob and I really hit it off that night. Before the evening was over, I was holding one of Jacob's business cards in my hand and had an offer from him to join his beach resort as a bartender for the summer. I drove out to the Breakwall the next day, filled out the paperwork, and by the time the lunch crowd rolled in, I was behind the bar, running the show as if I had been there for years.

Within three short weeks, Jacob had promoted me to manager of operations for the Breakwall. The responsibility for hiring, firing, ordering, training and security were all on my shoulders. During that summer with Jacob, I worked seven days a week, eighteen hours a day, with most of my compensation paid in cash.

Not that the move to the Breakwall was without conflict. While my rapid rise was a major ego trip for me, it offended many of Jacob's more senior staff. Whispers and dirty looks surrounded me. It took the better part of the summer, but I eventually won them over, mainly by staying above the attitude and just working hard. Through it all, it felt as though Jacob was testing me to see how I would handle the negativity thrown my way.

I guess I passed the test. My "just a summer job" became an "every summer job" for the next three years. During the long college breaks and each summer, I would come back to Buffalo and spend most of my waking hours in Jacob's employ. There was a small bedroom next to the office where I spent many nights, sleeping at the club instead of challenging my exhaustion and risking the long ride home. I rarely saw my family, and the only friends I had time for either worked at the club or came out to visit me there. As for female companionship, well, it was Peggy or no one at all.

The huge Breakwall sign and flashing neon palm trees loom over me as I try to gather the courage to move my Nikes to the next step. The last time I was here was the August before my senior year of college, almost two years ago.

At the end of that last Saturday night, I went from bartender to waitress to busboy to say my goodbyes. Jacob caught up with me and asked me to follow him out to the beach. When we got far enough away from the deck, he put his arm around my shoulder.

"So, David, my boy, this is your last night again?"

"It is, Jacob. I'm all packed and ready to head back to Fredonia tomorrow morning. I start classes on Monday and when the year is over, I'm off to Nashville to become the next Garth Brooks."

"What if I had a better option for you?"

"Better than being Garth Brooks?"

"I'm serious. What if I offered you a permanent position as bar manager with a big bump in pay, benefits, and the promise of it leading to you managing your own club? Would that be enough to keep you from going back to school? I have no doubt we could make big things happen, you and me."

"Jacob, I'm really flattered. But you know I've had this plan to follow my musical dreams to Nashville for years. Now that I'm only 10 months away from graduation, I can't turn away from that dream. I promise you, though, if my heart tells me that I belong at the Breakwall, I won't hesitate to call."

"I had to ask. I hate goodbyes, but especially now that you've become such an important part of this operation. I wish you a lot of luck. I mean that. And I had better hear from you – a postcard from Nashville, at the very least."

"You have my word, Jacob. I hate goodbyes, too. You've been a great friend to me." And with that, along with one last hug, I walked off the beach to the Jeep and never looked back.

Yet here I am, back again with my hat in hand. I had told Jacob that if anything changed, I would call, but I'd also promised to keep in touch, and we hadn't connected since that night on the beach. I'm not even sure if he'll talk to me now, let alone take me back. At this point, I would start out as a bar back if that's what it took. With my foot in the door again, I could climb back up the ladder.

So why can't I move off this step? The truth is, if this is my Plan A – a shaky one at best – what's my Plan B? What if Jacob tosses me on my ear? What if some other up-and-coming superstar has taken my place, maybe even the guy who took over when I left, and is outperforming every memory of me? I don't want Jacob to think I'm needy or desperate. C'mon, Davey. Where's that confidence, that bluster that has always served you so well? Probably beaten down by my Nashville experience. No time for that now. How good would that rush of being in charge feel right this minute?

I've gotta do something. I definitely can't stand here all afternoon.

Taking the next two steps in a single stride, I once again see everything the Breakwall has to offer. The winter clutter had been cleared from the beach, the driftwood stacked in the pit, awaiting the summer bonfires. The volleyball courts are ready and the lifeguard towers sport fresh coats of paint. Tables with striped umbrellas line the court area between the deck and the break wall. Wide steps lead from the deck to the courtyard and from the break wall to the beach. It is hard to imagine that mini-icebergs had floated past this beach on their way to the Niagara River and the Falls just six weeks ago. It feels like I never left, never went back to school and never headed south to Nashville, chasing a dream that never became a reality.

Visions from that last summer once again stop me in my tracks. I can see Peggy sitting at the table near the double doors, waiting for my shift to end.

Where did *that* come from? There's no way Peggy would come anywhere near this place now. I hadn't discriminated when I left Buffalo. Just as I'd not kept in touch with Jacob, Peggy hadn't heard from me since the week before graduation.

Peg and I met during my freshman year at Fredonia. She told me later she'd had a crush on me from the first day we met; it just took me two years to catch on. But once I did, you couldn't pry us apart. It seemed to go from crush to commitment overnight. When we met, her golden blonde hair flowed half way down her back. That soon gave way to a shorter cut that framed her round, freckled face and highlighted her greenish-blue eyes. We were a study of contrasts, but maybe that was part of the attraction for me. Her long, blonde hair and my short, dark, curly head; her light skin and my dark complexion. At 5'2" she was nearly a foot shorter than me, but that provided me with my favorite image of her, leaning against me in my arms, looking up at me with a smile that could illuminate a stadium. Never in my life had I loved or been loved so deeply. The picture of her looking at me melted my heart and at the same time haunted me through my many lonely nights in Nashville. More than a few tears were shed on those nights, knowing I had no one to blame for the loss of her but myself. What I wouldn't give to feel her arms around me again, one more kiss, one last candlelit night.

We would talk about the future, marriage, and kids constantly. But in truth, my heart wasn't totally in it. If I jumped into Peggy's dreams, it meant an end to my music fantasy. She told me often during our last few months together that she wouldn't wait for me if I went to Nashville. She saw it as an end, but I saw it as a beginning. I didn't view it as a choice between music and a white picket fence. Music could make both our dreams come true. But if I were forced to choose between Peggy and my dreams, Peggy didn't stand a chance.

I push past Peg's favorite table and watch her smile fade in my mind's eye, regretting what might have been. The more time passes, the more I miss her.

Standing now at the gateway to Jacob's kingdom, I feel the cool air drifting in from Lake Erie against my back. Nature's air conditioner. The Breakwall was Jacob's first club and it was his home. It had become close to the same for me, too. And it hadn't changed a bit.

The main room is darker than most beach bars, with only one wall of glass facing the deck and beach. The walls and floors are a natural dark oak with high tables and stools near the bar and shorter, square pedestal tables for more formal dining scattered throughout the room. The stage occupies one end and shares the space with a DJ booth overlooking the ample dance floor. This is the larger of the two stages, with its junior at the far end of the deck. Closed umbrellas hang among beach towels from around the world; a scattering of surfboards, a canoe, some oars, buoys, stuffed seagulls and other summertime paraphernalia decorate the walls. One section near the bar is dedicated to Jacob's true love – the Buffalo Bisons, the city's triple-A baseball team. He never misses a game and considered himself their number one fan.

Jacob had grown up in the bar business. His father had a small joint in the Old First Ward of Buffalo. He allowed Jacob to help out every weekend, mopping the floors, chopping up ice, cleaning the windows, sweeping or shoveling the sidewalk and restocking the refrigerator and bar. When he finished his work, he loved to sit on a stool at the far end of the bar by the wall and listen to the tales spun by the regulars. The bar business was in his blood. As Jacob often said, "I was born in a bar, and I'll probably die in one, too." His clubs were his family – his wife and children all rolled into one.

The centerpiece of any Horlansky property was the best-stocked, best-laid-out bar in the business. There was no such thing as being out of anything. You always had the mixers you needed, a customer's favorite beer and the perfect glassware and garnish for the quintessential presentation. And presentation was my specialty. That was one of the big reasons Jacob loved having me behind the bar. I was his best student, and he knew I always had his best interests at heart. He taught me how to move a customer from a well drink to the top shelf because that's where the big money is made. Jacob drove the idea of making a profit into my very being. The Breakwall had introduced its own privately brewed beer, and it became the top shelf for beer drinkers. I learned early on that being a bartender in one of Jacob's joints was not for the novice. His lead man was the heart of his operation. For four summers, I was the lead man at the Breakwall, and it was a perfect fit for me.

What I love the most about the bar business is the people – well, most of them. I have an ability to make magical connections with people with little effort. There used to be club regulars who would wait for me rather than give their drink orders to anyone else behind the bar. Most of the time, they didn't even have to give me their order. I remembered what they'd had on their last visit and would ask them if they wanted "the regular." I made them feel wanted, appreciated, like they were the only customer in the room. Jacob would sit at the end of the bar and marvel at the customers, old and new, who would seek me out, as if they all had the most important moment of their life to share with me. I tried never to let them down.

Nothing has changed at the Breakwall. Everything about this room is as I had left it. The music sounds the same, and the smells from the lake mix with those of a busy bar, as always. As I take it all in, a wave of nervousness washes over me. What if Jacob blows me off in front of his staff, many of whom will probably recognize me? I wouldn't blame him if he did – I deserve it. Friends don't blow off friends the way I did him. I feel guilty for having cut everyone out of my life, but especially so with Jacob. He'd given me the education and opportunity of a lifetime. Maybe it isn't such a good idea to meet with Jacob after all.

I start to back out of the bar, hoping no one will notice. I turn as I reach Peg's table but am startled by a bellowing roar of laughter that fills the room. Only one person in the world laughs like that. I turn again, glancing back at the bar.

Sitting on his self-appointed throne, the last seat at the bar by the wall, just as it was when he was a kid at his dad's joint, is Jacob. He is dressed for the season in sandals, white cargo shorts and his trademark Hawaiian shirt. Both arms extended, he is refereeing an argument between a waitress and a bartender over who was responsible for the total disaster of a drink order. It is obvious that the bartender is about to lose. Of course, it is equally obvious that the argument is less about the drink order and more about the floundering relationship between the bartender and the waitress. Every summer at the Breakwall, there are at least three love affairs going on at any given time. That was one merry-go-round I never set foot on. Jacob loved the idea that I was a one-woman man, and that Peggy was that woman.

Jacob's staff is very important to him. He is successful because he surrounds himself with people he trusts. You never wanted to be the reason Jacob had to leave a baseball game early, especially the Friday night bashes complete with fireworks. His love of fireworks came in a close second to the Buffalo Bisons for Jacob, and they became a staple of the Breakwall's Saturday night parties.

Jacob always seems to be on the hunt for trustworthy employees to add to those he already has on his staff, and I think he was on a hunt the night he found me. The more responsibilities I took on, the more he piled on me. Partly because he trusted me, but also because I think he was encouraging and flattering me into staying on full-time to become part of his permanent team.

The staff squabble has quieted. I watch Jacob retreat back to his throne and I begin to wonder how different my life would be today had I said yes to Jacob's offer two summers ago. I know I could have been running my own club by now. Peggy and I might be settling into a house in the 'burbs with a family on the way. Instead, I'm stuck in place, my feet glued to the floor in the middle of a bar, wondering where my next dollar will come from.

I glance back at Jacob. To my surprise, his eyes are locked on me. With all the backlight from the beach, I must be nothing more than a silhouette to him. He edges off of his stool and starts moving slowly across the bar, trying to change the angle of the lighting on me. But slow and stealthy is not Jacob's style. He puts too much weight on the back of a stool and it topples over with a resounding crash. We both start laughing.

"Will you cut it out?" I sputter.

"It is you!" he yells as he starts running toward me. For a wild moment I consider side-stepping him and watching him run right past me out onto the deck, but I am laughing too hard to move. The bear hug is inevitable. He pulls back, looks up at me and asks a question only Jacob could ask. "Are you here, or just here?"

I can't remember ever seeing such a smile on Jacob's face. He is waiting anxiously for me to say something, and I don't have the heart to make him wait. "I'm here if you'll have me, assuming your last offer is still on the table."

His smile disappears as quickly as it had arrived. He places two hands on my chest and pushes me away with all his weight. I stumble backward, hitting the small of my back against Peg's table. Jacob's sudden mood swing takes me by surprise.

"To tell you the truth, I don't know whether I should hug you or hit you," Jacob bellows with a rare fire in his eyes. "I can't believe I haven't heard from you in what – two years now? I thought our friendship meant something to you. Even if I had a spot for you, how do I know I can trust you now?"

He grabs me by the arm and pulls me back across the bar to the corner stools. For Jacob, this is his home court advantage. If he is going to negotiate, he is going to make the most of every factor.

"I don't know what to say. You are definitely more than just a boss to me. You are a friend and a mentor. I really can't apologize enough for all the mistakes I've made, Jacob. 'I'm sorry' doesn't even begin to cover it, but is it enough to get us started again?"

"Yeah, but just barely enough," Jacob says as he cautiously looks me in the eyes. "So, first things first. Why are you here? What's happened since…whenever?"

"You want to hear it all right now?"

"If you want me to trust you again, I do. I need to know why you disappeared for two years and if I can trust you not to disappear again."

So I start my story at the beginning. My senior year, my trip to Nashville, the mistakes I made, and the people I hurt. I tell him how the cocky, confident kid who left to fulfill his dreams, came back humble and scared, not knowing where his next steps would take him. My unbridled confidence had taken a thorough beating.

Jacob studies me like a bug under a microscope. I can feel his eyes boring into my soul, looking for the man I'd become. I know enough about Jacob's past to know he won't judge me. But I also know he is a businessman who makes decisions with his head and not his heart. I want him to believe me and see that I have changed. Jacob is still searching my face, looking for a sign that I am the old David, the one he trusted – and could trust again. With my autobiography complete, I nervously return his stare in silence. Then I see the beginnings of a smile on his face. I guess he found what he was looking for.

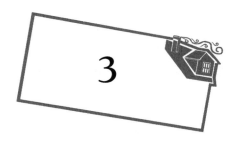

The Accident

JACOB OFFERS ME A WEEK to find a place to live and get settled before I start work again. I talk him into letting me move into the small bedroom in the club so I can start immediately.

When I report for my first day at the Breakwall, Jacob already has a plan laid out. I am going to work the service bar to give me a chance to brush up on my skills, get to know the staff and learn any new concoctions that are popular with the college kids. Within a week, I move to the main bar. Once again, I settle into my role as star of the show. By the middle of July, I have the run of the club and the one thing no other employee possesses – my own set of keys. A gift of trust from Jacob.

It is the middle of the baseball season and, with Jacob spending time at the ballpark, I find myself handling everything except signing the checks. A good bar is a currency printing press for its owner; a great bar is the equivalent of a gold mine. The rule for any such gold mine is to stay one step ahead of the employees and two steps ahead of the IRS. Jacob feels comfortable leaving me in charge. He knows I learned from the best – him.

My first night on the main bar, with Jacob perched on his personal stool, my readiness to take over the bar is tested to the extreme. As the band is finishing its second set, the lead singer steps off the stage to take her break – right into the arms of an inebriated patron. That doesn't sit too well with the band's manager, who also doubles as the lead singer's boyfriend. With an early-twenties crowd come beer muscles and bad judgment. This has the scent of a barroom brawl with the band and its followers on one side, and the local regulars on the other.

My signal brings the bouncers to the dance floor and the bartenders out from behind the bar. Safety in numbers, Jacob always preached. Another signal sends the waitresses behind the bar to keep an eye on the cash registers in case things get ugly.

My expertise in negotiating isn't doing much to calm the participants, so we jump right to the next and final step. The bouncers escort the battlers out to the beach to keep any damage to the bar to a minimum, while the lead waitress calls the local sheriffs. They are on the beach in less than two minutes. Two bouncers stay for the arrest while the rest of the staff return to their posts. As I walk back toward the bar, I can see that Jacob hasn't moved an inch. He is wearing a broad smile as I get closer.

"See, I told you that you were ready," he says, smirking. All I can do is shake my head as I walk past him.

"Thanks for all your help," I reply.

"You did fine without me," he laughs. We are both back in mid-season form.

I stay at the Breakwall through the end of September. Then I move to The Embers, Jacob's upscale club. The Embers attracts a consistently older crowd throughout the year. By the time I make the move, my bar skills let me do so without missing a beat. I find it easy to move from the young crowd to the 30s and 40s set. Martinis replace beer taps, Cosmos trending over craft brews. The mirrored wall behind the bar holds bottle after bottle of flavored vodka; the lower shelf carries the well brands and the top shelf stocks only the elite brands. Just as I did at the beach, I manage to keep moving people to the top shelf without effort. Before long, I am creating a whole new set of regulars seeking my attention.

By the time fall fades into winter, I pretty much have the run of the place. During his rare visits to The Embers, Jacob always comments on how smoothly I have moved between the clubs, from one crowd to another. Business has never been better. The banquet room is booked almost every night for the holiday season, and every banquet ends with a mass migration of guests to the main bar. That's when I get to wave my magic wand over the crowd and make each customer feel as if I am there to serve only him or her.

Christmas at a Horlansky club is the best time of the year. The little kid in Jacob can't spread enough holiday cheer throughout his bars. The regulars know this, and Jacob never disappoints anyone when it comes to Christmas parties and bonuses. I'd heard the tales each year, and while I'd helped during holiday breaks from school, this is my first full-time experience of a Jacob Christmas. And few things are better than the sight of Jacob in a Santa suit with the pant legs rolled up short enough to fit him.

It is the Friday night before Christmas, and I am cleaning the bar as the rush ebbs. Jacob calls to me, motioning me to come to the end of the bar where he's been camping out all evening. "David, I know you're working during the day tomorrow, but what are you doing tomorrow night?"

"I'm not sure yet. I'll probably be around. Why?"

"Because I want you to join me for dinner tomorrow night. I have a few things I want to discuss with you. How about when your shift ends, we grab a table in the back dining room? That way we'll have a little privacy."

"Sounds like a plan, boss. Is this black tie or are work clothes good enough?"

"It will be come as you are. You know I'm not dressing up."

Jacob is not quite 5'6" and not an inch of him is trim or fit. His hair, usually controlled by a baseball cap instead of a comb, makes you instantly think of hobbits. We figure we're lucky if Jacob shows up with something on his feet. Formal wear is definitely not part of his wardrobe. His invitation surprises me, though. I can't imagine what he wants to talk about. Most likely, he just wants to review the progress I've made over the past seven months. And maybe a thank you or two and perhaps one of those Christmas bonuses I've heard so much about.

As my Saturday shift winds down, I see Jacob standing by the waitress station. He catches my eye and cocks a thumb toward the back room, then walks through the archway and out of sight. I finish my last order and motion to the bartender relieving me that I am done. As I enter the back room, I see Jacob has reserved his private table in the farthest reaches of the club. He is waving at me like a little kid on the school stage who has just seen his parents enter the auditorium. He sits down and directs me to the other chair, just in case I can't figure that out on my own. It is clear he doesn't want us to be interrupted and has so instructed the waitresses. He even orders our dinner before I sit down so we won't be disturbed.

Small talk accompanies the wine, appetizers and salad. While waiting for our prime rib, Jacob gets down to business. "David," he starts, clearing his throat, "your return to the clubs has made this the best damn year I could have ever imagined. So I think it's time we start talking about the future – your future."

I always enjoy it when Jacob tries to get formal. It's all I can do to stifle a smile. Formality just doesn't suit him.

"I've been scouting locations for a new club, and I think I've found just the place. There's an empty warehouse out near the airport that I think will be just perfect. I want you to be involved from day one, including the planning and design. And when the doors open, I want you to be the general manager. It will be your club to run, top to bottom"

His last words are like an ice cold bucket of Gatorade being dumped over my head. I am totally shocked. I swallow, but can't put a sentence together. A second swallow seems to help a bit. "Jacob, you've got to be kidding. I've only been back for seven months. You have other employees with much more seniority than me. Don't get me wrong, I'm incredibly flattered and would love the chance, but is this really what you want to do? Are you sure?"

"In all my years in the bar business, I've never been more sure about what I want to do. As far as the other employees are concerned, they'll stand and cheer when word gets out. You've earned their respect, and they'll be fighting for a chance to work with you. Listen, David, I'm tired of grooming young kids into seasoned veterans who walk out the door and open a joint right across the street from one of mine. Of all the young kids I've trained, you are the very best, and I would much rather have you with me than against me.

"I'm looking at an October opening. I figure you'll stay here until May and then move out to the beach for the summer. But through it all, you'll be planning the new club. By the end of August, you'll be there full time. I'm going to stick with a winner, so I'm calling it The Embers II. I'll have my lawyer draw up a contract for us – a partnership agreement."

"Partnership?" I go from shocked to flabbergasted. "You are kidding now, right?"

"No, I mean it. A partnership. It will stipulate my guarantee to make you a legal partner in the club. Your commitment to Embers II is your part of the down payment. So what do you say?"

"I'd be a fool to say no, Jacob. So what's next? A handshake, high five, bottle of bubbly?"

"How about all of the above?" he said with his classic laugh, drawing the attention of every waitress and busboy in the back room. "Oh, and before I forget." Jacob reaches inside his cardigan and pulls out a thick envelope. "Merry Christmas, my boy!"

I take the envelope and crack open the flap to find a thick wad of bills with nothing less than a $20. My jaw drops. "Jacob!" I exclaim.

"Not a word." He responds with his finger to his lips.

And with a smile and a handshake, our new partnership begins. But little did either of us know at that moment just how short it would be.

It is barely two weeks later, on New Year's Eve, and I am helping out at The Embers. The party is one of the club's largest events, and the regular bartenders are getting crushed. As I run from one customer to another, I see a familiar face staring at me across the high gloss, ebony bar. I take an order for two specialty martinis and, while filling it, I try to put a name to the face. The drinks done, I return with two glasses but no answers. As I lift his $20 off the bar, I look at him one more time. "I'm sorry, man. I usually have a great memory for faces. I know I know you, but I can't come up with your name."

"David, it's Donny – Donny McShay. We're cousins once or twice removed. We used to spend the day together every year at the family reunion, but you haven't been at a reunion in years. It's great to see you again."

"Oh my God, Donny, now I remember you!" As a kid, he'd always picked me first to be on his softball team. He could hit a ball a mile, losing liners into the trees. "How have you been?"

"Couldn't be better. You remember Danielle, our youngest? She's about to leave us with an empty nest, and as much as I thought I would be dreading the moment, I'm actually looking forward to it."

"Hey, that's great. Is she off to college?"

"No, she's getting married in less than a month to a really great guy. Come to think of it, maybe you could help us out. We just found out yesterday that the bartender we hired has a conflict and can't work for us that night. Would you be interested in being our bartender for the night? We'd love to have you. Keep it in the family, so to speak."

"You know what, Donny? It's been a while since I worked a wedding, but it might be fun. Here's my cell number. Give me a call when you can with all the details, and I'll try to work it so I'm free."

It takes a couple of days for Donny to get back to me, and by then I've already decided I'll make it work for him. I've always looked up to him despite the small amounts of time we've spent together. I got a lot of my athletic confidence from his encouragement at our family softball marathons. But more important, it would be a one-night break from the endless marathon I'd been running for Jacob. I feel as though I've been going non-stop since Memorial Day weekend without a break. Any down time is quickly filled with Embers II details.

Donny gave me all the details of the wedding, including how many would attend. I'm curious because, although Donny is family, we aren't very close. But if it's a huge wedding, my parents might just be there. When Donny says they're expecting fewer than 200, I figure it's unlikely that my folks will be there.

I should have called my parents long before this – as soon as I returned. It's just hitting me that I've been back in town for seven months. But I'm just not ready for all of their questions, the deserved dressing down Jeannie would likely give me and another in a long series of conflicts with my father. Besides, I'm so busy at work, it's just been easier to stay hidden.

The Saturday of the wedding arrives quickly. I like to get an early start on private parties, and today is no exception. It's important to have plenty of time to set up the bar to my liking. I rummage through my belongings at the Breakwall and find my travel bag that I'd put together for all the private gigs I used to do. There is an extra shirt and tie, my own set of tools, mixing glasses, shot glasses; in fact, it's my own portable bar that ensures I'll never be caught short. Part of this is my own obsession and part is Jacob's training. His "be prepared" attitude makes me feel like I'm back in Boy Scouts.

I carefully place the bag into the back of my Jeep, jump in and turn the key. No response. Two more turns don't improve the situation, my forehead quickly joining my two hands resting on the steering wheel. After promising Donny I wouldn't let him down and looking forward to getting out of my rat race for an evening's celebration, I just have to get to the reception. I can't disappoint him.

I think about calling a tow truck, but instead, I call The Embers. I ask for Jacob, but he hasn't returned from running some errands. The best I can do is Melanie, the restaurant manager. She says she'll check with the staff and see what she can come up with. She calls back and says that Chris, one of the newer bar backs, will pick me up. I can take Chris back to the club and then go on to the reception. I'll get back long before the end of Chris's shift and can take care of the Jeep in the morning. A few minutes later, Chris pulls up in his Ford Crown Vic. There is no doubt that this car is an ex-police cruiser – big, long, heavy and all black. A Crown Vic isn't my choice of cars for a Buffalo winter foray on a night when heavy snow is predicted, but I have no other choice at this point. The last thing any self-respecting Western New Yorker would do is make or change plans based solely on weather predictions. Lake effect storms are predicted all the time, but they don't always materialize. I transfer my travel bag to the monstrous trunk of the Crown Vic and take Chris back to The Embers.

The reception is at the American Legion post in Wheatfield, north of the city. I'm not enjoying the ride at all. The accelerator is touchy and this land yacht seems to want to go from 0 to 60 instantly. Add rear wheel drive to the equation and the Crown Vic wants to fishtail with just a slight touch of the steering wheel. I pull up to the drab brick building with its center entrance surrounded by flags. Slinging the duffel over my shoulder, I head down a hallway with plaques and pictures covering the walls. Legion members in a variety of uniforms – including softball and bowling – fill the frames. I feel like I should be enlisting instead of tending bar. Walking into the large event room, the oversized bar comes into view at the far end of the room, with cases of liquor along the wall. I get to work setting up everything the way I like it, marking my territory.

Although I am used to a fast-paced, active bar, I don't expect a busy night at this wedding. Even so, I am not prepared for just how relaxed and low-key the reception is. Of the 200 or so guests, fewer than 50 approach the bar for a drink all evening. Yet the room abounds with laughter, dancing and conversation. All the traditions are covered, from the first dance by the bride and groom to the father-daughter and mother-son dances. The band, loud but not very good, manages an eclectic hit list including the Hokey Pokey and Shout, as well as *Hava Negila*. I am surprised at the lack of bar activity, but amused by the atmosphere. Since the pace at the bar leaves me with time on my hands, I watch with great interest as the reception moves along.

I decide to take a quick break and get some fresh air. I step into a small hallway near the restrooms. A group of women is gathered in the hall. Two of them look up. One of them is my Aunt Lucy. She taps the shoulder of a woman with her back to me and points in my direction. She turns quickly. It's my mother. I guess my guest-counting analysis wasn't so accurate after all. It takes her a moment to realize that she is looking at her son. She starts to move toward me, slowly at first, but quickly picking up her pace until she is sprinting and nearly jumps into my arms. She buries her face in my chest and holds me tight. I can feel her try to catch her breath between the sobs. Despite how sure and confident I usually am, I find myself speechless in front of my mother, whom I haven't spoken to in almost two years. Mom is equally speechless. The awkwardness gives way to a hug only a mother would have for a lost son, one watered by both our tears. Mom pulls away first and then looks up. I turn, too. Dad has walked up to us, but does not join the hug. He looks a bit older, but otherwise the same: a rock of a man with broad shoulders and a thick neck. He has former Marine written all over him, still keeping his haircut high and tight, as they say.

There is no smile between us, no obvious emotion at all. He sticks out his large hand. "David."

My hand is engulfed in his. "Sir." We stare at each other in silence for what seems an eternity, with Mom looking back and forth between her two men.

I finally break the silence. "Look guys, there's so much I need to say, but I'm the only bartender here tonight, and I have to get back. It's a pretty slow bar, so if you guys want to come by and talk, you're welcome to." With that, I turn to head back to the reception, trying to hide my tears.

It takes Dad less than 10 minutes to find his way to the end of the bar. I can feel his eyes on me, watching my every move. I turn to him and attempt a smile, asking, "What are you doing?"

"I'm just amazed at how much you've grown over the last two years, how much you've matured. When all you have is memories, it's hard to visualize the person as who they are today."

"Dad …"

"Son, I'm not looking for an explanation about where you've been. Your mother and I are just thrilled you're back in town. All that matters now is what happens tomorrow and the day after that. Are you back to stay?"

I hesitate at first. Of course I am in town to stay, but I don't know how Dad will feel about having a son in the bar business – and not just in it, but a bar owner. He isn't against drinking, but he doesn't like bars as a place to do it. I don't want to start an argument, but if I am going to rekindle any kind of a relationship with my family, I'm not starting it on a lie.

"Dad, I'm back working with Jacob and have been since last May. In fact, he's opening a new club in the fall and I'm going to be his partner and run it as though it's my own." I can't miss the wince on Dad's face at the thought of his son spending his days and nights in the less-than-holy atmosphere of a bar. I step away for a moment to serve a guest. As I walk back to Dad, I see him staring intently at the floor. "Dad, you OK?"

He looks back up at me, his eyes clearly moist. "I was just thanking God for answering our prayers. Our family was incomplete while you were gone, David. We always believed – had to believe – that you would come back. Faith made it come true."

Well, that didn't take long. Dad's faith has reared its ugly head and that familiar feeling of discomfort has me shifting from foot to foot. Once again, Dad has managed to place God squarely between us. This is exactly why I stayed away for so long in the first place. And once he gets started, Dad is like a Baptist preacher with no end to his sermon in sight.

"Dad, you know your religious devotion has always been a sticking point for us. Please, just let it go."

"David, my faith gives me the strength to go on even when I don't know where I will end up. But I trust the path I'm on. And I know God has a path for you with great things ahead of you."

I feel like a bear caught in a trap. I scan the room just to avoid eye contact with Dad and with the guests accumulating at the bar, waiting for service but happy to listen in to Pastor Tom.

"Dad, please stop!"

"Your travel down that path, David, is on God's time, not ours. My faith allows me to turn this over to Him and not worry about the results. Your faith isn't there yet, but that doesn't mean God can't use you. You'll reach a crossroad in your life when you'll need to rely on your faith to show you the way. You'll know when the time is right."

Now it's my turn to wince as a smattering of "amens" and "halleluiahs" come from the crowd that has gathered around the bar. My foray into the hall and the attention to the conversation with Dad seems to have backed up the crowd at the bar.

"I can tell that your hearing hasn't improved since I left. I asked you to stop." I hustle back to the guests, hoping they will get their orders and give us some privacy. But even with their orders filled, few leave the bar, wanting to hear how the sermon will end. I move reluctantly back to Dad's pulpit.

"I love you, son, as we all do. I'm proud of the man you are and believe in you. Come home for dinner tomorrow night, David. The only way the past two years will come up is if you want to talk about them. You have my word."

I take a deep breath and let it out, moving hesitantly into Dad's outstretched arms for a hug – to a small smattering of applause from the crowd. Aunt Lucy has moved front and center with her hands clasped to her chest, a tear or two adjusting her makeup.

"Thanks, sir, dinner sounds great. I'll come by around five," I answer.

As Dad walks away, I look across the hall and see Donny watching the whole scene. He is leaning up against a pillar with his arms crossed in front of him, seeming very pleased with himself. It suddenly occurs to me that none of this was an accident. Was Donny so manipulative that he managed to make this scene happen? Did he really lose his bartender or did he relieve him on purpose to choreograph this father and son reunion? I don't suppose I'll ever really know, since it's clear by the smug look on Donny's face that he isn't about to come clean.

Throughout the rest of the evening, I find myself thinking about Dad's sermon. While I pack up my belongings at the bar, I wonder if I'll be able to make it through a family dinner without getting into another debate with Dad and ruining the evening for everyone.

I throw my duffle over my shoulder and head for the front door. As I approach the foyer, I see my mother waiting for me. Her arms are crossed and her eyes follow my every step. Mom is a petite, pleasant woman, but she is not someone you want to cross. She is afraid of no man, and that includes her leatherneck husband.

I open the inside door and she opens up on me with both barrels. "Listen to me, mister. Don't let my joy in seeing you tonight mislead you into thinking that you are in any way forgiven for what you have done. Your father just told me that you have been back in town for more than half a year. Is that true?"

"Yes, ma'am."

"How could you do that to me? To your sisters? What have we ever done to you other than love you? Just because you can't be decent to your father is no excuse for you to throw us all away, to not even take our calls. If you come to dinner tomorrow night with anything less than a full-throated apology for all of us, including your father, then he's not the one you will have to worry about. I will personally throw you out the door, and don't think for a second that I can't. You have hurt us all very deeply and that's not how you were raised."

"Mom, I..." She doesn't wait for me to finish. She storms out the door and climbs into the car next to my father. They pull away, neither of them looking back.

Despite being uncomfortable whenever Dad gets into his pulpit, I have fond memories of my days growing up in the church. As I load the car, I think about all the friends I made, the lessons I learned. I try to pinpoint when it all started to change for me, what it was exactly that started to move me away from my faith and from God, but I can't remember that clearly. The one thing I do remember is telling Dad about these changes. He told me that if I find myself farther away from God than I used to be, it wasn't God that had moved away, it was me.

Out in the American Legion parking lot, I brush the snow off the Crown Vic, get the engine started and pull onto the snow-dusted street, heading back to The Embers. As I back drive along the I-290, my thoughts wander, wondering again what it would take to make peace with my family. I can just imagine the look in Mom's eyes were I to stroll into church one Sunday morning, the corners of her mouth turning up and her eyes softening the way they do when she's proud of her kids. I am picturing that look on her face as I crest an incline near the Colvin Boulevard exit and hit a patch of black ice.

Maybe it is my unfamiliarity with the Crown Vic, or perhaps I'm not totally focused on the road, but that tank of a car starts fishtailing into a full skid, sliding down the road sideways and slowing down slightly. I pull my eyes from the windshield and glance at the driver's side mirror in time to see an eighteen–wheeler on top of the rise. That object was definitely closer than it appeared in the mirror, and there is no chance the truck will be able to slow down or stop.

The truck closes in on me in slow motion, with the driver's side door absorbing the brunt of the impact. I hear the glass shatter around me, but that is all I will remember. I don't feel the car break away from the front bumper of the huge rig, nor do I feel the old police cruiser slam into the side rails along the expressway. I never hear the Jaws of Life the firefighters use to cut me out of the crumpled wreck or see the doubts in the faces of the EMTs that I would even make it to the emergency room. But that is probably just as well.

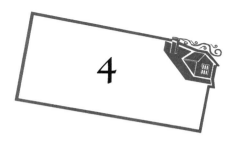

4

Along for the Ride

M*Y SENSES ARE ON FIRE, fanned by extreme pain, but I can't respond. Sirens wail inside my head. Voices bark instructions. Needles stick into my arms and straps hold my body against the hardness of a board.*

I want to scream, but I can't. I want to look at my surroundings, but my eyes won't open. My body won't do anything I ask of it. I remember the eighteen-wheeler's headlights growing bigger and bigger in the window and then the impact.

This can't be happening to me. I have too much to do, too much life left to live, *I scream inside my head. I have to get out of here!*

More orders are yelled out, another needle. I am sinking into the backboard. Am I just relaxing or am I dying? Oh God! No, don't let this be the end.

Then, suddenly, I'm at peace. My eyes aren't open, but I can see. A young man all in white is near me. He looks down at me and smiles. He holds a long, hooked stick, resting it against his shoulder.

I sense a hand on my shoulder, but it's not one of his. I sense a presence, too. Peace radiates from that touch, comforting me. A bright light gets closer, illuminating the visions, pulling me in. The pressure from that hand on my shoulder grows, and now it's two hands, four hands, lifting me up as the light dims and a feeling of safety overcomes me.

Suddenly, I feel the cold winter air and people are moving the board I'm on. But now I feel as though I'm floating above it. The pressure of that hand remains and so does the young man who moves with me as darkness claims me from within.

I know my life is in the hands of others, some real and some merely sensed. I feel cradled within those hands as sleep overwhelms me.

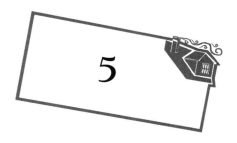

5

Origins

*F*ADING IN...FADING OUT.

How is it possible to feel everything going on around you and yet be totally detached from your body? Hard to understand, harder yet to explain. I can hear but I can't respond. I can sense my body parts, but have no control over their movement. I can think, dream, imagine and remember, but I can't make a sound. Doctors and nurses hover over me, inject, probe and bathe. Visitors tend to me and talk to me and respond to me as if I have responded to them. They tell me secrets that would mortify them if they knew I could actually hear them. They pray over me and read to me, yet I can neither thank them nor join in their amens.

The doctors call it a coma; I call it hell.

I have heard people talk about being near death and having their whole life pass before them. A coma is similar, but my life is taking its time displaying itself. It's sort of death in slow motion. The dreams are in Technicolor and tend to drift from moment to moment. The memories come intact with the emotions I felt as they happened, and they are so real that it is like reliving them over and over again.

I am back in Nashville. I feel a soft, warm breeze drifting in through the only window in my studio apartment. The two candles burning on my nightstand dance in the wind, casting animated shadows across the ceiling. They are the only light in the room. I lie on my single bed, staring at the designs above me cast by the candles. This is most definitely not the way I had pictured my Nashville adventure. In my fantasy, there had always been the stage, a microphone, a stool, and smiling faces crowded into the room, enjoying every song I shared and applauding enthusiastically. But it just hadn't turned out that way. Once I got to Nashville, my fantasy met cold, hard reality head on.

I didn't handle this trip well at all. On graduation day I gave Mom and my sisters big hugs, there was a handshake for my father, and then I jumped in my already packed Jeep and headed south to Nashville. Even though I always enjoyed being the front man in a band, I saw my future as a solo artist. Nashville is a city rife with success stories. I thought that people with talent went there and hit it big. But I discovered that it's really not about talent at all. It's about circumstances, luck and destiny. While luck was not the only thing out of my control, it was the most important thing, and the best performers have to learn to deal with that. I convinced myself that I had to give this my absolute focus and dedication for one full year. Even if I saw just a little movement, a small taste of success, I would extend my stay in Nashville beyond that year. But if I was still just sitting at the starting line after twelve months, I'd head back home knowing that I had, at the very least, given it my best shot. I never pictured coming back home empty-handed. I just knew it would work. Ah, the optimism – or inexperience – of youth.

Hands are on me, rolling my body. "Can't let this guy get bed sores," one of the nurses sings. The movement doesn't interrupt the dream.

My definition of absolute focus was the first of my many mistakes. Absolute focus to me meant cutting all ties with my past: family, friends, Jacob – even Peggy. I distanced myself from everything and everyone that had been my life.

One night I was thinking about the many lonely nights I'd been spending staring at dancing shadows on my ceiling, wondering why I was walking this path alone. Was I really pursuing a dream or was I just running away from a life full of conflict? Was I using this move to Nashville as a way to avoid my father's obsession with guiding me down the "right" path?

My family was the center of my life. My parents created a warm and comfortable home for me and my sisters. Jeannie was two years younger than me, and Hannah was another two years younger than Jeannie. Hannah was happiness itself; she never seemed to be without a smile on her face. When we were kids, she followed me wherever I went. I can see her sitting on my lap as I read to her at night, watching our favorite movies, and swimming in the above-ground pool in the backyard. As we got older, I was her go-to guy, her idol. If she had questions or concerns at school, I was the one she went to, not Mom or Dad.

The closeness I shared with Hannah frustrated Jeannie. She saw herself as second in command to Mom when it came to running the house. If I made a mess, she was just as likely to yell at me as Mom was. She was no-nonsense. Jeannie's attitude carried over to school, where she was class president from whatever year you start voting for such things until she went off to college. She was a natural-born leader, yet those leadership skills created a distance between her and everyone else that she found difficult to overcome. Whenever Hannah and I started giggling, Jeannie would storm out of the room.

Mom decided to go back to work when Hannah started first grade. She applied for the secretary job in the town clerk's office, and to her surprise, she got it. Adding her salary to the family coffers created a more comfortable lifestyle for all of us, as well as the time and means to make family a focus. It was a tough adjustment at first for Mom, but once she settled into her job, she kept things at home running smoothly, with chores done and dinner always on the table when Dad got home. We pitched in a bit more, but most of the helping fell on Jeannie's and Hannah's shoulders, since I always had after-school activities that got me home just before Dad arrived.

Once Dad walked in the door, tensions started rising, at least for me. I can see his cold, hard face, his flat top haircut and his steely eyes as he sat down for dinner. It was almost as though he was sitting at attention while he ate. His communication was limited to please pass whatever he needed next. If I tried to talk to him, I was ignored. He made me feel as if I were the least important being in the world. I remember walking into the house one night, dragging my backpack behind me. He snapped, "What's wrong with you?"

"I just got cut from the basketball team," I responded.

"What did you expect?" he mumbled.

What did you expect? What did you expect? What kind of father says that to a son? It was like sticking a knife in my stomach and twisting it. Even in this coma, I can feel the wound he left behind, still bleeding all these years later.

But it hadn't always been like that. I remember spending lots of time with him when I was little. Dad was a police veteran in my hometown of Tonawanda. He had worked his way up the ranks to captain, earning the respect and admiration of his peers and superiors with his dedication. But he somehow always managed to leave the job at the police department when he came home. Until the year I turned eight.

I heard the story so many times while I was growing up that it's almost as if I had been there. I even remember reading the copy of the police report Dad kept hidden in his desk. It was a Saturday morning shift, and Dad, a patrol officer at the time, was near the Sheridan Parkside projects when an armed robbery call at a 7-11 on Sheridan Drive came through. Dad arrived just as a kid ran out the front door of the store. It was clear he was carrying a weapon in his hand. Dad cranked his cruiser hard into the parking lot, used the car door for cover as he jumped out of the vehicle, and ordered the young man to stop. The kid stopped and turned, firing two rounds that slammed into the windshield of my father's cruiser. Dad returned fire, still shielded by the car door. His first shot missed, but the second found its mark in the center of the gunman's chest, guaranteeing that the young man would never become an old man.

Dad came out from behind the car door and approached the kid cautiously, his gun still fixed on the motionless body. He kicked the gun lying beside the victim's body out of reach and began radioing in as he checked for a pulse. There was none. He stood motionless over the body for a few seconds and then returned his weapon to its holster. A second police cruiser arrived. Dad told the officer to stay at the scene while he went in to talk to witnesses inside the store. Suddenly, Dad heard a scream from the apartment building next to the parking lot. A young woman was hanging out a window begging for help. Dad raced into the building and the open apartment door, and tore into the bedroom where the woman was screaming. There, on the floor in her pajamas, was a young child, no more than five years old. She was lying amid an ever-growing pool of her own blood. For the second time in minutes he checked for a pulse, with the same result. He rose and turned to the shocked mother, hugging her against him.

As with any shooting, Internal Affairs took Dad's weapon and assigned him to desk duty during the investigation. He was cleared of any wrongdoing, and the death of the child was determined to be the result of that first errant shot from his Glock – collateral damage. Patrolman Hynes, however, never saw that young girl's life as just collateral damage. From that day forward, he was a changed man.

At home, he spoke little. Our time together disappeared. I had never before seen Dad cry, but it was a sight I became very used to. Mom did all she could to support him, but nothing seemed to help.

The singing nurse is back, gently changing bandages around my eye, cleaning the wound as she hums her way through her assignment.

I remember the day that changed everything one more time. Dad found something that pulled him out of his funk. After almost a year, he started attending church. The pastor's words gave him some peace, and he was drawn to the concept of being forgiven for all of his transgressions by a loving God, finding even more comfort in that forgiveness. His vision of the dead little girl on the floor slowly became a painful memory instead of totally consuming him. Unfortunately, at least for me, the peace Dad found was something he wanted all of us to share. He insisted that we become as involved in the church as he was. If it had fixed him, it would fix all of us.

He expected us to attend church with him twice a week. We began saying grace before every meal, and instead of just saying goodnight to each other, Dad wanted us to gather for a family prayer at the end of every night. At first, it was new and exciting. After all, this was what had brought back the Dad we knew and loved, so we all went along with it. Mom, in particular, jumped in with both feet. She and Dad were baptized together at the new church, but the girls and I rebelled against that idea. God was supporting Dad through this tough time in his life, and apparently Dad wouldn't be happy until each of us found the same help from God that he had. He was relentless in pushing his faith into our lives. But the harder he pushed, the more I pushed back and the faster I ran away.

The older I got, the more I resented these changes in my father. I couldn't understand how my hero, the strong, tough cop, could give up control of his life. It changed my whole vision of him. I was even jealous of the time he spent with God. Mom seemed to be caught in the middle. She wanted Dad to be happy and comfortable again, but she saw that what was working to heal him was hurting the family. The distance that Dad was creating between his faith and his children kept increasing. What ripped the family apart ripped Mom apart, too. Every time she saw the gulf between Dad and I widen, she suffered anew. The wider the gulf grew, the louder our conversations became. And every mistake I made, every setback I experienced and every girl that turned me down brought back the words of my father from years past that never seemed to leave my head. "What did you expect?" Echoing, haunting, piercing.

So once I had the excuse of going to Nashville, it was almost a relief to use it to cut my ties with my family. People who haven't spent time in a very religious family or a born-again church just can't understand what it's like. No one at home listened to me or took my dreams seriously. The more they bashed my dreams, the more I avoided them, staying at school during breaks or at the Breakwall if I came home at all. It was hard enough to climb Mount Nashville without my parents as ankle weights, pulling me down. In the beginning, I tried to keep in touch with Jeannie and Hannah. But every time I called them, Mom eventually got on the phone and it started all over again. I'd had a great relationship with my sisters, but I ended up having to shut the door on them, too. It wasn't fair, but I didn't see any other option. The longer we were separated, the harder it became to try to fix it. When Hannah called, I found myself letting her go to voicemail.

When I arrived in Nashville, I decided Memorial Day of the following year would be my drop dead date. I poured myself into making my career happen. I worked constantly on new songs and improving my act, but I soon began to run out of venues that would give me stage time. I'd sold a couple of songs to help maintain my meager lifestyle, but there wasn't much interest in my presence on stage. I did the open mic circuit, hoping for the break that never seemed to come.

There are moments when this coma feels as though it might be about to end. Sparks of life, flashing lights, like lightning streaking across a summer sky. Then, as suddenly as they come on, they end, settling me back to my cell of sleep and my never-ending dreams.

One of the two candles has burned out and the second is sputtering now. The shadows on the ceiling darken. In the tiny apartment, nearly all available floor space is filled. But there's still plenty of room for loneliness and regret, and I'm well stocked with both. Part of me wants to pack up before the second candle burns out and head back home, but another part of me doesn't want to quit just yet. In truth, I've never felt so alone. Even in the worst of times back in Buffalo, Hannah was never far away if I needed her.

One thing I'd learned that I still didn't totally understand was that I needed to be connected to be happy – and successful. While I still looked forward to every show, I had started feeling out of place up on stage, uncomfortable. Weird. I loved being the front man in high school and college and never experienced more than a minute of stage fright. But it's not simply the butterflies in Nashville; it's that the butterflies are so big they could wear saddles. I just wasn't connecting with the audience any more. My small talk was falling flat, my jokes even flatter, and by the end of the gig, I wanted to be anywhere but on that stage. My frustrations caused me to strike out at the people I needed the most. I developed a reputation among club owners. The more they rejected me, the angrier I got. I was thrown out of more than one club. I slowly realized how small the club owner community was, how much they talked to each other. It had become apparent that my name was coming up, and not in a positive light. My opportunities were quickly dwindling.

All of which makes my room more of a cell on death row than the creative space I thought it would be. The only thing hanging on my walls is a calendar with the months passing by in slow motion. As April became May, I began to hear the executioner's steps approaching. I lost my appetite and got very little rest; deep sleep got to be pretty rare. An evaporating dream takes its toll on mind and body. When you finally have to acknowledge it's gone, you feel like you'll never smile again.

The Memorial Day drop dead deadline was right around the corner, and dropping dead is exactly what I felt like doing. Night after night through the month of May, I calculated the costs I'd incurred chasing my dream. Not the financial ones, but the personal ones. Was the past year worth losing Peggy? Will I ever find someone to fill the hole she left in my heart?

And what about Jacob? Can I possibly save that relationship? Will Jeannie and Hannah even talk to me? Will Mom understand? What about Dad? If I go back, will he and I pick up where we left off or will he be able stop pushing his religion down my throat? Maybe I don't have to worry about any of this, I remember thinking. Maybe I've done too much damage and I'll never be able to fix any of those connections from my life in Buffalo.

Sunday of Memorial Day weekend was my last show and my last chance. My legs were heavy as I climbed onto the stage. I worked my way agonizingly through my hour-long set, ending it with only polite applause from the audience and a sigh of relief.

Truth be told, I was actually looking forward to packing my Jeep the next morning for the return trip to Buffalo. But once I was behind the wheel, I had to admit that the 700 miles between Nashville and Buffalo was a road I really didn't want to have to travel. The mile markers beat by rhythmically like blips on a heart monitor, bringing me closer and closer to an embarrassing homecoming, announcing my utter failure. Not only that, but I still had no concrete plan for what to do with my life. The B.A. I earned from Fredonia wouldn't get me far, and I wasn't about to pursue another degree. The closest I could get to a plan was to reconnect with Jacob to see if he might have a place for me back at the Breakwall.

I see myself pulling off the New York State Thruway and heading to the beach. A parking place is waiting for me right across from the main deck. I jump out of the Jeep and have a good stretch after the long ride. Heading for the first step, my left foot freezes just as I lift it. The Breakwall's neon sign is flashing down at me with its neon palm trees waving in unison. I can hear the waves beating up on shore, but to my ears, it sounds like a dream smashing to bits. Well, the next stage of my life has to start some time. Wipe the slate clean, pick up a piece of chalk and write myself a new dream.

New dreams, old dreams, lightning flashes again across my memory screens. Bouncing from painful memories to the crushing reality of this coma. Voices, hands on mine, machines breathing for me, feeding me, charting my every heartbeat. When will it end?

Fading out...fading in.

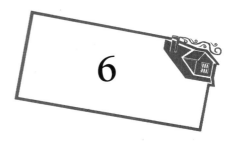

6

The Road Back

I FEEL AS THOUGH *I am floating on a cloud among the lights of the trauma unit, looking down on my broken body. My face is a perfect substitute for a Halloween costume, and my body is limp and has been since they pulled me from the mangled car. Facial trauma, cuts, a broken nose and at least one broken cheekbone were the highlights from the neck up. I also had blood trickling from my ear, I was unconscious and my breathing was shallow. And these are just the visible injuries.*

My mind floats back to the accident, exposing mental snapshots the wreck left behind. I'm amazed I survived it at all. The rescuers had to cut the roof off the car to remove me. They had to slash away the seatbelt, without which my ride would have been to the morgue and not the hospital. Not a single window was intact, and the gas tank had split, spewing fuel all over the highway. It was a miracle that nothing caught fire. The most amazing thing is that the huge Ford engine, after crashing through the firewall, had come to rest on the passenger seat beside me — not on me. Yet another miracle.

Mom and Dad take turns keeping vigil by their damaged son. The girls also spend as much time with me as possible. I can't talk, open my eyes or acknowledge my visitors, but I am aware of each reassuring voice. I have always been an active, athletic, non-stop kinda guy, and here I am, for all to see, a living mummy, hanging on to my life by the thinnest of threads. My visitors have to peer past a web of wires and tubes just to watch my chest rise and fall to verify that I am still alive and breathing.

I can hear the doctors and nurses talking to my parents about my condition. They say I had originally been placed in a medically-induced coma, but that my own body is now keeping me in that state. If there is pain, I can't feel it. The doctors say I did well in the second surgery, which stopped my cranial bleeding and relieved the pressure on my brain. I can feel the machines moving my chest to keep me breathing…something to do with a collapsed lung. One of the doctors also mentions "spinal shock." Apparently I'm not paralyzed, but he did sound concerned about it. The next seven to ten days will be crucial.

Clearly even the doctors don't know I can hear every word, or they might be more careful about what they are saying. I hear one say there's only a 10 to 20 percent chance I'll survive and even if I do, I might have brain damage and will definitely need months of physical and occupational therapy. I don't think he's right about the brain damage, though. I mean, if I had brain damage, would I be able to hear and understand every word spoken? This, at least, gives me some hope.

Despite all the dire predictions, Dad keeps the aura in my room upbeat. His constant prayers and strong faith are unshakable. Conversations with visitors are always positive, with Dad talking about the future that he expects will include me. Dad believes in nothing but my full recovery and will not allow anyone to challenge this belief.

Today must be a Sunday because I can hear Mom and Dad talking about what people said at church. I can also hear Jacob's voice. He's going on and on about me, what it was like to work with me, how I was the reason for all the increased business in the clubs and that I was also responsible for changing Jacob's life. This isn't the first time he has spilled his heart out like this since my accident. It's so out of character for him. If only I could move – I'd punch him in the arm for embarrassing me. Suddenly Jacob jumps off the side of the bed. "Tom, he grabbed me!" Dad saw the movement too, and called out the door for the nurse.

Colors. I can see colors and bright lights. The flashing bolts of lightning are back. I can feel my eyes fluttering, trying to open.

"We're here, baby!" It's Mom, calling out to me as she grabs my hand. I can feel her tears drop onto my hand as my eyes close again and my world grows more peaceful, calmer. It only lasted for a moment, but I want more.

This scene repeats itself several times over the next few days, with fewer tears from Mom. The doctors must have determined that I was coming out of my deep sleep. They start removing some of the wires and tubes each day. It is like coming to life a few minutes at a time, with each period lasting a bit longer than the last. Then, alone in the darkened room, my eyes open but don't close again. Minutes later, a nurse comes in to check my vitals and finds me looking back at her.

"Well, hello there, mister. Can you hear me?" I know that voice. It is the singing nurse. I smile and nod back at her. The breathing and feeding tubes had been removed a few days earlier, but a small oxygen tube is still under my nose. "Would you like me to move the bed up a bit for you? Give you a chance to sit up?" I can hear the motor start to lift my head to a new view. The rising sun is breaking through the window, and the light of day never looked so good. The nurse props me up on my pillows and straightens the blanket on my bed.

"Thank you."

"Oh, you're up for talking, too. You are entirely welcome." She squeezes my hand and leaves the room. She comes back with a plastic cup containing water and a straw. "Let's see how this goes down. Take very small sips at first."

Just then, Dad walks into the room. He had probably figured on a quick visit before going into work. Since he is in uniform, none of the staff care that he has arrived before visiting hours.

"Hi, Dad." He stops dead in his tracks and stares at me. Then a smile lights up his face and the tears start. He leans over me and gives me an awkward hug, whispering in my ear.

"Thank you, Lord!"

"How long have I been here?"

"David, it's been four weeks. The doctors have been more encouraging each day. I'd say they are cautiously optimistic you'll make a full recovery. It was really close for a while, but I knew you wouldn't leave us. They said your spine is good, and your legs have started to heal nicely. But they're still concerned about your head."

"Yeah, that's always been my concern, too, going all the way back to first grade"

Dad's laugh fills the room and spills out into the hall. "I guess the doctors can scratch long-term memory loss issues off their list. Do you remember anything about the accident?"

"Bits and pieces. Colvin Boulevard keeps coming back to me."

"That's because your accident was only about a hundred yards from our house."

"Small world, huh?" Dad and I talk for a while longer, but I feel myself getting tired. Dad says he has to go to work anyway, but that he'll stop by later on. He kisses me on the forehead as I start to drift off.

Gradually, my strength returns. Time truly seems to be the best medicine. Every day I cross thresholds that bring me closer to a full recovery. Doctors come in groups to discuss my case. Apparently, I am a modern medical miracle, healing at a rate no one expected. Nor can they believe how little permanent damage I am left with. I am truly becoming as good as new, despite the doctors' belief that I was lucky just to be alive. I am Erie County Medical Center's Miracle Man.

I am surprised how quickly my memory is returning. I can finally remember every moment of the accident. In fact, my whole life seems to be in sharp relief. I remember my commitment to Jacob and our contract terms down to the penny. I remember the discussion with Dad at the wedding reception. I even apologize for not making it to dinner the next evening. I feel I am catching up on the time I lost in the coma.

The biggest advantage of being alone in my hospital room is the amount of time I have to think about my life, about how I had gotten to this point. It is something I clearly need. It's hard to think of the accident as a blessing, but I can't deny that it is turning out that way. Coming back to town as I did, jumping right back into work at the Breakwall, I hadn't taken any time to rebuild the relationships I had left behind. In fact, I did everything I could to avoid them. Now, being stuck in this bed is giving me plenty of time to consider the damage I'd done to the people who meant so much to me. And not just time to reflect, but time to do something about it, to make amends.

Mom and Dad spend most of their time with me, and as my release date approaches, I feel Mom and I have reached an understanding. She never again brings up the conversation we had at the wedding. Dad and I manage to stay in the same room without fighting, so that is progress. Of course, I can't exactly run away anymore

Peace comes quickly with Hannah. As the baby, she is the most forgiving. She listens intently as I explain my actions and ask for her forgiveness. Hannah is the family peacekeeper; she just wants everyone to be happy. During my coma, she sat by my bedside and read to me. She talked, held my hand and carried on as if I heard every word. Little did she know that I did, but I knew it would embarrass her terribly if I ever let on. Now that we can talk, we pour our hearts out to each other and grow closer than ever.

Jeannie, however, is an altogether different story. She is making no effort to hide her anger at her big brother. Jeannie is a protector, not a peacekeeper.

"How could you abandon us? Do what you did to Mom and Dad? And what about Hannah? You were her idol. We didn't know if you were dead or alive. It's the most inconsiderate thing I've ever seen. Who, exactly, do you think you are?"

"Jeannie, I..."

"I don't want to hear it. There are no excuses and no apologies for this one. I just want you to get well so I can kick your butt. You deserve a good beating. I don't care what issues you have with Dad. What you did to Mom and Hannah was just downright cruel." It seems strange to me that she never counts herself among the wounded.

It goes on like this for weeks. It is quite some time before Jeannie can spend time with me without renewing her attacks. But once she gets it all out, she is finally able to listen to what I have to say and accept my long list of apologies, making one thing very clear: "If you ever pull anything like that again, I will not be so forgiving."

Jeannie also has news for me. "I ran into Peggy yesterday. She heard about the accident but couldn't bring herself to visit. David, she is seeing someone and it might be serious. I just thought you would want to know."

Jeannie's words bury me in an avalanche of memories. With those memories come many regrets. Somehow, the accident makes the thought of settling down more attractive, and there had never been anyone else in my life I would have considered settling down with.

I know that I love Peg and that what we shared was real. I am beginning to understand that another reason for running away to Nashville was the fear that my love for Peggy would make me sacrifice my dreams. A part of me had hoped she would wait for me. But she hadn't. This is my biggest regret of all.

Jacob is, by far, my most enthusiastic visitor. He comes by three or four times a week, always arriving with an armful of floor plans and pictures of Embers II. For Jacob, it is full steam ahead. Nothing has altered his original plan. He believes that through sheer force of will, he can have his partner back on his feet in no time at all. Amazingly, this ridiculously positive outlook is contagious. He is like a leprechaun, jumping from pictures to blueprints to list after list of things that have to get done. He turns every visit to my room into a party. As my energy returns, I am, for the most part, right there with him, matching his enthusiasm. I pore over the plans with as much intensity as he does, making suggestions, modifying the blueprints, proposing lighting plans and a computer system to sync and track the cash registers. Jacob resists the electronics at first. He'd learned at his father's knee that the bar business is a cash business. Why track your profits and have to pay taxes on all of them? But he trusts me and wants me to have free reign to run this club as I see fit, and I value Jacob's trust more than anything else.

Yet through it all, I feel like a fraud. I am disappointed to admit to myself that over the last few weeks in the hospital, I find I am acting the role of an enthusiastic partner with Jacob, not really feeling it. I am unsettled by acknowledging that, but I'm not sure why. Because of my friendship and trust with Jacob, I want to bare my soul, but I'm not sure he'll want to hear what I have to say. I don't want to hurt him, but I have a haunting feeling that my life is not on the same track as it had been before the accident. I can't put my finger on exactly what track it will be, but I know a change is coming, as if something is hovering over me, watching me and about to tap me on the shoulder. It is almost like I am about to be held accountable, but for what I don't know. I don't want to burst

Jacob's bubble until I have some rational explanation for this sense of foreboding.

While I still don't have complete recall of every second of the accident, certain scenes are perfectly etched in my mind. I remember begging God to give me another chance and promising to serve Him if that chance arrived. People always promise to devote themselves to God when asking for a huge favor, and most of them never follow through once the crisis is over. But I find myself revisiting that particular moment again and again. Oddly, the more time passes, the more committed I feel to that crisis-motivated promise I made to God. I now have that second chance, and I want to do right by it. Is there a connection between my desire to honor my commitment and this feeling of impending change?

My hospital stay provides long, uninterrupted stretches of time to review where I have been, what I have done, and what I should be doing to move forward. The time forces me to face the demons I have created in my life. Jeannie's words hit me the hardest – who *did* I think I was? To have walked away from everyone in my life without a word was cruel and selfish. Maybe being *that* person was what got in the way of my music career, kept me from finding the success I had dreamed of. Because if I wasn't comfortable with me and if I was not feeling good about who I'd become, how could I convince complete strangers to believe in me, bet on my number, when they had so many other choices? Instead of gathering people to me and my dream, had I been chasing them away? Having now spent time rebuilding some of those damaged relationships I'd left in Buffalo, I am seeing the person I've always wanted to be. It centers me and brings me an inner peace, a feeling that I'm finally on the right track. Looking at myself in my hospital mirror, seeing my injuries, I see myself anew. I find it amusing, in retrospect, that my room in Nashville had no mirror at all. This is just as well. Who I was in Nashville was not someone I wanted to examine very closely.

It is a snowy Friday afternoon in early April, close to the end of the day shift, when "my" medical staff gathers in my room along with Mom, Dad and Jacob.

The trauma doctor who manages my case, Dr. Fisher, speaks for those assembled. "Mr. and Mrs. Hynes, all the physicians involved in your son's case met as a team this morning. We all agree that it is time to send David home."

Mom is absolutely beside herself. She doesn't know what to do first: hug Dad, run to me, or hug the doctors. Flustered and torn, she throws her arms around a surprised Jacob. "Can we take him home tonight?"

"We would prefer to keep him here over the weekend," says Dr. Fisher. "The team will use the time to finalize prescriptions and referrals for physical therapy, future appointments, and monitoring. We don't anticipate any dietary restrictions, but we would like to monitor him for the next 72 hours before we cut him loose. We want to err on the side of caution if we are to err at all. I'm still amazed that he is going home as soon as he is. David's activities will be restricted for the next four to six months so everything can heal properly. He might opt for some plastic surgery after the facial injuries heal, but they can wait until we see how things progress."

Jacob fills glasses with water from the pitcher by my bed, hands them to all those present. "A toast," he says, "to David. Homeward bound at last!"

"Here, here's fill the room, drowning out Dad's amen.

This snowy Friday brightens considerably with a start date for my new future – one full of hope and surprises yet to come.

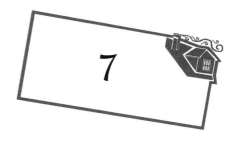

7

Collection Time

MONDAY MORNING CAN'T COME QUICKLY enough. The weekend is spent making plans for my release. I will move back home with my family until my recovery is complete. I plan to hold off returning to work for at least two more weeks; more, if I'm not confident I am strong enough to handle the hours I need to put in behind the bar and planning for Embers II. Jacob optimistically circles the two-week date on his calendar, but I am already thinking it could be longer than that. I don't want to push too hard and wear myself down.

I already have another appointment on my calendar. My parents are planning a welcome home party the following Friday night and will host it in the church hall. Knowing my parents, the list of invitees will be lengthy.

When Monday morning dawns, I find myself alone and excited to be leaving the hospital. My breakfast tray is already gone, and I am standing beside my bed packing memorabilia into a box that Sandy, the singing nurse, has supplied. I think about the multi-month recovery that the trinkets I am packing represent, taking time to reread a few of the cards I haven't looked at in a while.

"Good morning," says a voice from behind, startling me.

I turn and see a young man about my age at the foot of the bed. "I'm sorry," I say slowly, "I didn't hear the door open."

"It didn't," says the young man with a peaceful smile.

"Excuse me? What do you mean it didn't open?" I ask, examining the visitor more closely. I quickly realize that this man is not a hospital employee. In fact, I'm not sure exactly who he is. He is dressed in white from head to toe. His dark hair lies casually across his forehead. His arms hang loosely and his hands are clasped. Tucked inside one arm and against his shoulder is a long stick with a large hook at the top. All in all, he appears far more comfortable and at peace than I am feeling at the moment. I realize that the room seems brighter somehow, as though fresh light bulbs with increased wattage have been placed in all the lamps.

"David, I have been sent as a messenger to you, to collect a debt which you have incurred. The time has come."

"A debt? I thought my medical bills were being settled by the insurance company."

"The debt of which I speak has nothing to do with the financial cost of your stay; it is a cost for the brevity of your stay." He comes around the bed and draws closer.

"Brevity, what do you mean brevity? What are you talking about? Who are you anyway and how did you get in here?"

The visitor draws closer yet. "Your doctors have told you that your recovery is nothing short of a miracle." He reaches up and places a hand on my shoulder, and as he does so, the room grows even brighter until the bulbs seem to flash and explode, showering me with piercing sparks. The extraordinary heat from the sparks penetrates my face, my back and my legs.

He comes around behind me and I feel him place both hands on my shoulders. He gently guides me to the mirror on the wall next to the bed. "Have you looked at yourself lately?" he asks. "Have you not thought what the source of such a miracle might be?" I am unable to make a sound. When I see the image in the mirror, when I see no scars around my eyes, no sign at all that an accident has ever occurred. I leap backwards in shock, only to find that the visitor is now in front of me, facing the mirror. My leap should have knocked him over, but instead I have passed right through him. It's as though he does not exist. Is he real or just a vision? Whatever he is, one thing is undeniable: my scars are gone. I have not only been healed, I have been made new again.

He turns to me again. "My name is the same as yours, and my Father has sent me to collect on your promise. I am a simple shepherd and have come to gather the lost lamb. You asked the Father to save you, not to let you die, and if He did, you promised to spend your time serving Him in repayment. Do you remember this?"

I remember my prayer as though it were yesterday. I stare at the visitor, still only inches away, trying to make sense of his words. Yes, I remember my promise to God that night, and yes, I've had a feeling for some time that something new and different would soon come into my life. But this – this is way beyond what I expected.

"The Father takes such contracts very seriously. And He knows you will honor your commitment. He heard you, knowing you had arrived at your crossroad."

"So how do I repay this debt? What am I supposed to do?"

The visitor walks to the foot of the bed. "As I have done, you are to gather the flock. Bring them back to safety. Show them the path that has been set out for them."

"That's the best you can do? That doesn't tell me a darned thing. Is going to church more or teaching Sunday school sufficient? I suppose I should have been more specific, but I was dying. I guess I left a few open ends." I throw my hands into the air as I pace in a small circle. I turn back to the visitor. "How am I supposed to find these lost sheep? Where are they?"

"How you do that, young shepherd, is your decision. As for where, you will travel a long road, leave your family behind, and seek out the lost sheep."

"Hey, wait a minute. Leave home? I can't leave home," I say. "I just got back. I have a life here now, people who depend on me and plans that have been in the works for months. A boss who just invested in me big time. I can't just walk out on everyone again. No one will understand. Heck, even I won't understand."

"The Father has provided no other options. And your departure must not be delayed."

"I don't get it. Don't tell me there are no lost sheep in Buffalo. I could name dozens of people who I know personally who are absolutely clueless. Why do I have to leave again?"

"As it says in the Word, a prophet is least respected in his own village. To complete your task, you must leave."

"Oh, so now I'm a prophet?"

"My task here is complete. You now know what lies ahead of you. The Father has planted the seed of a plan within your heart. I cannot supply you with any more guidance than I already have. All you need do is allow the seed to grow and follow your heart. A crossroad only exists when the traveler decides to follow another path and then acts on that decision, and it is time for you to act."

I turn back to the mirror to examine my face one more time, my nose almost pressed up against the glass. Just then, another flash of light fills the room.

And with that, he is gone – and again, the door never opened.

I run to the window and tug at it, but it is closed tight. I pull up the edge of the blanket and look under the bed, but see nothing. I race to the bathroom and pull open the door and find it empty. I look again in the mirror, seeing my scar-free face. I pull up the leg of my jeans and look where my shin bone had burst through my skin, leaving a long scar. My leg is as pristine as it was before that snowy night.

I run to the door of my room and literally jump into the hall, looking in both directions for any sign of my messenger. He is gone, completely gone. Standing at the nurse's station, in his long white coat, is Dr. Fisher, handing a chart to Sandy. I sprint down the hall, skidding to a stop in front of my trauma surgeon, startling him.

"David, pushing the envelope here, aren't we? I thought I told you to take it slow."

"Doctor, I need to ask you something," I blurt out.

"Shoot," replies the doctor.

"You did the surgery on my broken leg, right?" I ask while breathing heavily.

"Yes, I did. Why?"

I pull up my pant leg again. "This leg, right?"

"Yes, David, that leg," said Dr. Fisher as he glances down at my exposed shin. But his glance becomes a double take as my healthy leg comes into focus. He takes his reading glasses out of his top pocket and drops to one knee for a closer look. Holding my calf in one hand, he examines every inch of my leg. He slowly looks up at me, his mouth open, speechless. He looks like a shoe salesman waiting for the answer to a question.

"Please, doctor, give me some medical explanation of how this could have happened. Not just my leg, but my eyes and forehead too. Look at me," I plead. "Tell me you have seen this before."

Dr. Fisher rises again, examining my sudden lack of facial wounds, shaking his head, Sandy watching his every move from her nurse's station. "David. No, I can't provide any explanation for you. I have never seen anyone heal like this. It's impossible. Maybe we should keep you a few more days to take a look at all of your procedures…"

"Sorry, Doc. I've been here long enough. Besides, I think I already have the answers I need. This goes way beyond any medical miracle."

Three feet away, Sandy stands with her eyes closed, her head bowed and her hands outstretched to the ceiling, singing as she is prone to do. "Praise the Lord!"

Praise the Lord indeed, for messengers and miracles. I have only one question: now what?

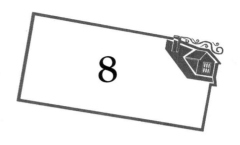

Surprise Party

THE RIDE HOME IS QUIET – too quiet. I can tell that Mom is uncomfortable with the silence. We had become close again during my hospital stay, and this is the longest stretch of silence since I'd come out of the coma. I am a million miles away this morning, staring out the passenger window as streets, cars, people speed by. I am deep in thought.

"Davey, does being back in a car again make you nervous?"

"No Mom, I'm OK, just a lot on my mind. It's not the car, honest." It really isn't. Nor is it her. I keep staring out the window, running through my experience with the mysterious visitor. I think I should be confused or scared or frustrated or maybe even apprehensive. But I'm not. Instead I am at peace, more peaceful than I've been for years. It is almost as if I had expected that visit. That feeling of disquiet that had been my constant companion throughout my recovery has disappeared.

Of course, I still wish I knew more about what I am supposed to do. Apparently, this position doesn't come with a job description or instructions. It comes with nothing more than a clean slate. All I know is that I have to serve, and that I have to leave town to do so.

My visitor also confirmed what I'd known for a while but was reluctant to fully accept. I have been healed, just not by doctors. I won't need physical therapy now, or any further checkups.

But now what, indeed? How do I follow such vague instructions? Do I share this experience, this special gift with anyone? How could I not tell everyone who had prayed for my recovery that their prayers had been answered – in spades? Or will they all tell me that it's my damaged head playing tricks on me, or that all the medications are taking their toll? How do I convince them otherwise when I'm not totally convinced myself? The doubt is still there and I have nothing to act on short of my faith, propped up by the miracle healing. For now, what little faith I have will have to be enough.

I keep thinking of my father's references to God's path. My visitor mentioned it, too. "Bring them back to the path." Dad was right on target from the beginning, but I know if I tell him it will just start another sermon. How, exactly, am I supposed to show others their path when it took me 24 years to just get a peek at my own?

"I am so not equipped for this," I say to myself as I stare blankly out the window.

Mom pulls into the driveway, but I don't even notice. I don't realize she's turned off the engine until she speaks. "Honey, are you OK?"

"Yeah, Mom, better than I expected to be, that's for sure." I glance from her face to the only real home I've ever known. I hadn't lived here for the six years between college and Nashville, but it hasn't really changed. I climb out of the black Chevy Traverse and go around to the back to claim my belongings.

"Oh, Davey, leave those," Mom said. "Your sisters and I will bring that stuff in for you." I look back and smile as I grab all three bags effortlessly and sling them over my shoulder.

"Mom, how about you just grab the box. I'm fine, really." I walk through the garage and into the kitchen. A fresh batch of Mom's cookies is sitting on the counter. So many memories come flooding back with their aroma. It is as if I have just gotten home from school and am heading upstairs to do my homework. My mouth watering, I snag a cookie on the way past, climb the stairs and walk into my old bedroom. What I see shocks me. Not a thing had changed in those six years. A package of peanut M & M's is sitting on my desk exactly where I had left it. Mom must have moved them a hundred times to dust and then put them back in the exact same spot. I smile at the thought of her doing that and then am sobered. What had she been thinking all those years as she preserved this scene?

I drape my bags over the desk chair and settle onto my twin bed. Despite all the questions running through my mind, I still feel at peace. I know little about what lies ahead, but one thing I do know is that my path will take me away again – away from family and friends. I know I will have to make a clean break of it. After all the time and care people have invested in my recovery, I wonder if I can leave a second time. How do I tell my parents and sisters that, with no specific plan in mind, I am leaving them again? How do I tell Jacob that, despite his partnership and everything we've already done together, I won't be around to make it all a reality?

The hardest part is trying to figure out how to explain my intentions. My visitor didn't say I couldn't tell anyone about what happened, but who would believe me? Mom and Dad, possibly, but then how do I explain it to others? I have to figure it all out before the party Friday night. That will be my chance to say goodbye to everyone. By Saturday morning, it will be too late; I will be gone by then. But for now, I need sleep.

My Monday afternoon nap turns into nearly 24 hours of very productive sleep. I wake up Tuesday morning with the semblance of a plan already in my head. Mom is planning a family dinner, and I am going to take that time to share what is in my heart.

Despite my head start on a full night's sleep, I am the last one up. Dad and Mom are already off to work, the girls at school. I am going to be on my own for much of the day, with no transportation and little desire to socialize. It seems like a good day for a long walk on the nearby Ellicott Creek bike path. I'm not sure I'm up for the entire 10-mile round trip, but it will be good to be outside with some time and space to think. The hospital room had become pretty claustrophobic. A day in the great outdoors will be a welcome change.

I grab a shower and rummage through the kitchen for breakfast. The refrigerator is packed with the lasagna and salad for dinner, but I find my favorite granola cereal in the cupboard, along with a cinnamon roll on the counter with my name on it – literally. I smile at the thought of Mom scribbling a Post-it note for the covered plate.

It's an uncommonly warm day for April in Buffalo. The snow of the previous week had melted, and spring is rolling in. I dress more for June than April, but keep a hoodie with me just in case the weather changes again. The bike path becomes more deserted as I head east along the blacktop trail. It follows the creek and cuts through open areas on the University at Buffalo's North Campus, staying far away from traffic and noise. Trees are beginning to bud, birds call across the greening expanse, and some early butterflies are bravely having a go at survival. It feels good to be alone with my thoughts in such a peaceful setting.

My upcoming journey is never far from my thoughts, but at least when I'm alone there's nothing else I need to be concentrating on. I come back to the quickly approaching discussion at the dinner table tonight.

"I know I have to tell everyone about my visitor," I say out loud to a passing squirrel, "But where do I go with this afterward?" The squirrel is of no help.

"And what do I say to Jacob?" I ask a goose who is keeping a watchful eye on her goslings. "He deserves to know my plans, and he deserves to hear it from me face to face, not as an announcement at some party." The mother goose honks in agreement, but her trailing chicks offer no words of wisdom.

I can't even begin to know how to tell Jacob about my visitor, my new mission, my completely unplanned future that will take me away from Buffalo – again. "And I can't even offer a guarantee that I'll ever come back to The Embers II, or even Buffalo, for that matter," I observe to myself. "I don't understand it myself, so how do I expect anyone else to, especially someone like Jacob, who's not very religious to begin with?" Saying it out loud doesn't help me come up with an answer.

Despite the peace my visitor has left me with, my guilt from my first journey still weighs me down. As an isolated event, changing plans and leaving Buffalo is not a big deal. This must happen to someone nearly every day. But when it happens after leaving the way I left two years ago, it feels as though I'm letting my loved ones down. I keep thinking that when I break the news, everyone's going to accuse me of running away again. How do I make them see my commitment to this mission? Make them understand that this time, I'm running *to* something and not away from anything? If only my visitor hadn't been so adamant about me leaving town. I would stay here and try and make everyone happy, spend more time with the girls, work fewer hours but stay committed to Jacob. Maybe that's why I have to go – so I won't be distracted by life.

I'm absolutely certain that, without God's intervention, I would be dead, not meandering alongside Ellicott Creek, talking to squirrels. That contract I entered into with God the night of my accident saved my life and placed me firmly on a path. Not my path, but God's.

As I think through all this, my pace slows. I stop often to sit on benches along the way, not because I need to rest, but because I want more time to think. I throw my hoodie over the back of a bench and sit back, allowing the sun to soak into my body for the first time this spring. Head back, eyes closed, a million miles away, deep in thought.

It feels good not to have to rush through this walk because I have to be somewhere or because I feel I'm taking time away from Peggy. What about Peggy? What would she say if she could hear my speech at dinner tonight? Funny how at a time like this, she pops back into my head. It feels like this is something I should share with her, but I also know that won't happen. She has no doubt written me out of her life. Despite that, she never leaves my heart, not for a minute

The growing peace inside of me is still strong and deep. I realize it's because I'm more comfortable with my decision, and have accepted the unknown tasks ahead of me. I feel strong, healthy and clear-headed. Quite different from how I felt beginning my journey to Nashville. I started that trip for fame and fortune. It was a "me" journey. But this new journey is all about God, with me being His servant, His shepherd. This is a selfless mission.

On those sleepless nights, alone in my room in Nashville, I'd thought about my place in the world, how I'd be able to tell if success were close by. I believed the true measure of a man was not the number of hit singles he had written, or the value of his car or the number of bathrooms in his house. It was measured by how many lives he had touched. I had always imagined my music touching others, but I had no way to quantify it. But this time, on this journey, I am the song – and the instrument. I am going to be the visitor, the messenger. Knowing that, truly believing it, is the center from which my inner peace comes. Doubts remain, but the more this mission gets under my skin, the more I realize that even the accident was no accident.

By the time I get back home, Mom and the girls are there. The aroma of baking lasagna fills the kitchen. Hannah has already set the table, and Jeannie is working on her laptop, supposedly writing a paper. I suddenly feel like I am at my parent's home, but it's no longer my home – that I am an outsider. To cover my discomfort, I sneak upstairs to wash up while Hannah works on the salad and Mom tends to the garlic bread. Dad will be home any minute and dinner always follows on his heels.

Tonight's dinner is the usual fare, unchanged since I last sat with everyone at this table. Dad says grace and remains quiet for the rest of the meal while the girls and I fall right back into our old roles, verbally poking at each other, interrupted only by Mom's occasional, "Kids, stop it." Dad is usually quiet at dinner as he mentally shifts from his stressful day to his family. For him, the ride home is never long enough to leave the cop behind. Tonight, as the girls clear the table, I ask him how his day had gone and all I get back is a blank stare.

He finally mumbles a response. "I got tied up all day dealing with some personnel issues, my least favorite thing to do."

I don't get the chance to follow up as Mom comes back with strawberry shortcake and enough whipped cream to blanket the driveway. As everyone settles back at the table to take on dessert, I clear my throat. "Hey guys, would you mind hanging around after dinner? I've got something really important I'd like to share with all of you."

"All of us?" asks Hannah.

"Yeah, Squirt, even you." I get four nods of agreement from around the table, followed by an awkward silence and a round of covert glances.

We move to the family room. Everyone grabs a seat but me. I stand quietly in front of them, looking and feeling awkward, with my hands clasped. I can't take my eyes off the magazines on the coffee table. I finally force my voice into the room.

"While I was unconscious, from the moment of the accident until I woke up, even though I couldn't move, my mind and some of my senses were working," I said. "I could hear everything anyone in my room was saying. My mind was working constantly. There was a moment, right after I first got to the hospital, when I knew that I was dying. In fact, I was certain of it. As I felt myself fading, I remember praying to God, and the promise I made if He saved me. I told Him,

'Father God, save me. Please don't take me now. I haven't finished Your work yet. I know you put me here to follow a path You set out for me. But I failed. Please, Father, give me a chance to redeem my life. I promise you, if it is your will to save me, then I will live my life to serve You. You have my word, if You let me live, I will live to serve You. I promise.'"

I look at each of their faces, trying to read their emotions. I shift nervously from foot to foot, anxious about sharing the story of my visitor, afraid they will think I really have suffered brain damage.

"While I was getting ready to leave the hospital yesterday, I had a visitor. He entered my room without opening the door. He seemed to brighten the whole room as if light were emanating from him. He knew my promise word for word, and he said my recovery was a miracle from God, not modern medicine. Then he told me I was being called to fulfill my promise. But he didn't say how or exactly what I was supposed to do. Even though I don't know what the exact plan is, I know what I need to do."

I take a deep breath and continue. "I need to go on a journey. Unfortunately, this will take me away from home again. I'm planning to leave Saturday morning." I stop and look at the faces around me. First at Dad, whose head is bowed in prayer. Then I move to Mom, who looks worried and is staring at me intently.

"Davey, you have been through a lot these past few months," Mom says. "You really shouldn't be making any major life decisions. You still have physical therapy and doctor's appointments you need to go to. This isn't a time for you to be wandering off again."

I walk slowly toward her. "Mom, look at me. I've been healed by more than doctors. I pull up the pant leg of my jeans. "Remember the scar I had here from the 27 stitches I needed? Can you see it? Can you see any trace on my body of the accident I survived?"

I kneel down next to her and take her hand in mine. "I have never felt better, Mom. But the doctors didn't do all of this."

I rise and turn to Dad. "For years you've been saying that God has a plan for me, a path. Well, I didn't just find my crossroad, I crashed into it. And just in case I couldn't figure it out for myself, God sent His messenger to make sure I understood. And no, I'm not crazy."

Tears spill from Dad's eyes and run down his cheeks. He rises from his recliner and pulls me into a hug, his tears soaking my t-shirt. As much as I want to return the hug, the friction that still exists there between us causes me to hold back.

Mom, in tears as well, joins us, but I can tell her tears are much sadder than Dad's. His are tears of joy that I've finally found God – or rather, God's messenger has finally found me. Mom's tears are those of a mother losing the son she has just gotten back. Mom, I know, will come around as soon as she sees my determination to make this work.

I turn to the girls who have been watching silently. "Jeannie, everything you said about me is true," I admit. "I was being selfish when I left for Nashville, and I don't know who I thought I was. This time is different. Not only do I know who I am, I know who I will be working for.

"I promise both of you that I won't disappear again – even if you want me to," I say with a smile. "I'll e-mail you every day to share my journey. And I will be back."

They jump from the couch and run to me, flinging their arms around my neck. There are no tears in this hug, just smiles and pride.

I step away from the girls and walk toward the picture window in the family room which looks out to the highway that had been built behind the house. I gaze to the west, where an oak tree used to tower, my oak tree, in the exact same place where a truck slammed my car into a railing and changed my life.

All I can do is shake my head at the miracle. My family, torn apart when I left two years ago, is reunited as the prodigal son returns, and now that I'm leaving again, remains united, sealed with a blessing from God. What they say is true after all – if you have faith, whatever good things you have lost will come back to you.

Yes, He does work in mysterious ways.

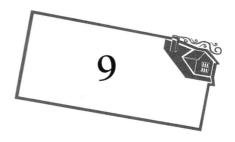

9

Let the Journey Begin

Friday night arrives in a heartbeat. The celebration at church is at 7:00, but I have a very important appointment before that. I called Jacob and asked him to meet me at the Left Bank at 5:00. This small, quiet restaurant in the heart of the city is somewhere we can talk without interruption. Jacob had pushed to meet at the Embers, but I want neutral ground with no prying eyes or ears. He asked if he could bring the plans for Embers II, but I told him to leave them behind. "All you need to bring is you."

If the long afternoon before I talked to my parents had been nerve-wracking, it doesn't hold a candle to waiting for my evening with Jacob. This is worse – much worse. I have no way of guessing what his reaction will be. And that's what worries me. Jacob has invested a great deal of time, energy and money in creating Embers II. In fact, he probably wouldn't have moved forward with it at all had I not returned and become his partner. I was the final piece that fell in place to make it all happen.

Falling out of that place will be the most difficult part of my mission. Despite the selfishness, which, I have to admit, was a large part of my year in Nashville, I do not normally take promises lightly. If I say I will be somewhere or will help someone, I'll do it. Walking away from the promise I made to Jacob leaves me feeling unworthy to pursue any path created for me.

I wait outside the Left Bank for Jacob, pacing to pass the time. The unseasonably warm weather continues, and in fact, it's downright balmy for April. I wear my best jeans and a plain white, long-sleeved dress shirt. I decide to wait at the corner of Rhode Island and Richmond so I can see Jacob coming from any direction. Punctuality for anything other than a Bisons game is not one of Jacob's priorities. But tonight he surprises me. As the bells chime from the church across Richmond, I can see Jacob plodding up the sidewalk. The sight brings an instant smile to my face. For the first time in my memory, Jacob is in a suit, though it fits him so poorly, he might have borrowed it.

"I've never seen you look so formal. It's a whole new you," I comment with a smile and my arms outstretched as he comes up to me. "No Hawaiian shirt? No baseball cap?" Jacob returns my smile and points down at the pavement. Peeking out from under the too-long pants, I can just see his old flip flops. I laugh and pull Jacob in for a hug. We walk into the restaurant with my arm draped across his shoulders.

The ambiance is perfect. Subdued lighting, art on the dark-brick walls, tasteful silk flower arrangements and baskets of greenery. A warm and welcoming environment. The bar is also impressive; only the finest labels are displayed.

The hostess seats us immediately. This is unusual for a Friday night, but it is still early. Our table is quiet and secluded, just as I had hoped it would be.

Jacob orders a Sam Adams Seasonal draft, but I decide to keep a clear head and ask for a Pepsi. Jacob updates me on all the barroom gossip – who's dating who, who's leaving for another bar, and who's leaving to open up his own joint. Then he starts telling me about the progress at Embers II and the ongoing battles with subcontractors. Our server interrupts us only briefly to take our dinner orders. I go with the Panko breaded chicken, and Jacob chooses his old reliable New York strip steak. Our salads arrive quickly, and the conversation slows as we begin to eat.

As the salad plates are removed, I clear my throat, "Jacob, I've got something very important to talk to you about." He looks at me with a hard stare.

"Well, the floor is all yours, my friend."

"Besides being my boss, you've become my best friend, Jacob," I say, looking directly into his eyes. "Your support and trust in me with the business, your concern while I was in the hospital, your confidence in my ability to make Embers II a success – it's been amazing. I can never repay you for all you've done for me."

"I thought tonight was supposed to be full of testimonials for you," says Jacob with a wry grin.

"I'm serious," I insist. "You've been my lifeline since I returned from Nashville, giving me a sense of stability I never imagined I could find here in Buffalo. Bringing me on as a partner in Embers II is more than I could ever have dreamed. I know how much you're counting on me, and that makes what I have to say to you so terribly difficult."

Jacob's grin disappears by the time I finish my sentence. "I'm not sure I like where this is going, David. You'd better get to the point."

"I'm leaving again, Jacob, and I don't know when I'll be back."

The words drop like rocks on the table and Jacob's stare could drill a hole through my forehead. "What do you mean you're leaving?" asks Jacob, his voice rising. "Do you have any idea how much I've invested in this club – in you?" His voice is growing louder and heads turn in our direction.

"You can sing your damn songs in the bar if that makes you happy," he huffs as he shakes his head. "I can't believe you're doing this again, David. I thought I could trust you this time"

"This has nothing to do with music," I assure Jacob.

"Really? Then enlighten me," he demands.

"I'm not sure how to explain it. I mean, explain it so that it makes any sense."

"Don't give me that, David. I think your 'best friend' deserves an explanation. In fact," adds Jacob, his voice tight, "your best friend is demanding one."

"Okay, but you need to really listen to what I'm saying, Jacob, not just hear the words. You were at the hospital almost every day. You saw every procedure I went through, every bandage going on and coming off. You even watched them remove the stitches around my eyes, right?"

Jacob nods.

"You still have that flashlight app on your iPhone?"

"Yeah," said Jacob, flashing me a puzzled look.

"Shine the light on my face, my left eye, and tell me what you see."

"And why am I doing that?"

"You gotta trust me on this. Just do it."

Jacob fumbles in his suit pocket for the phone and pulls up the flashlight app. He aims the beam at my face and frowns. He brings the light even closer to my face and is startled. He opens his mouth, but no words come out.

"That's how my whole body healed, Jacob, inside and out. There isn't a mark on me from that accident. My healing goes beyond medical expertise – way beyond. I am completely healed. Every scar, every pain, every ache is gone. I am strong, I am fit, I am better than new." He stares at me in silence, slowly shaking his head to clear the growing disbelief.

"And do you know how it happened, Jacob? The night of the accident, while I was fading in and out of consciousness, I prayed to God for the first time in years. I asked Him not to let me die, and I promised to do His will if He saved me."

I search Jacob's face, trying to see if he understands what I'm trying to say.

"He saved me, Jacob, body and soul. This is His work," I say, gesturing toward my body. "He answered my prayer, and now it's my turn to give back as I promised I would. I'll never be able to live with myself if I don't find a way to pay back this great blessing."

"And just how are you going to do that?" Jacob asks.

I look away from him for just a moment, shaking my head. My eyes move back to lock on his. "I don't know exactly. But what I do know is that I have to leave in the morning to fulfill my end of the bargain."

Jacob draws in a deep breath as his face darkens. He stares hard at the plate the server has just put in front of him, not even registering the generous steak and baked potato. Although he is clearly trying, he can't hide his anger. I can measure the effect of it on his face as his blood pressure rises. He looks up to find me staring at him, waiting for a response.

Suddenly, he leaps up, nearly toppling his chair behind him. He turns and strides purposefully across the restaurant, walking out the door.

I get up to follow, but stop myself at the front entrance foyer. I need to give Jacob some time to sort through all this. I look out the side window next to the door and see him standing right in front of me. I can hear him through the glass, talking and cursing to himself.

His eyes lift to the rising moon, he drags his fingers through his hair and curses loudly and creatively enough to make a sailor proud. A couple on the sidewalk, heading for the door, swing a wide arc into the street to avoid the lunatic ahead of them. Jacob continues his rant, cursing and kicking stones out of his way and tearing posters off a nearby street pole. He draws back his leg to kick the fender of a Lexus parked in front of the restaurant, but stops just before making contact. Instead, he rests his hands on the hood and lets his head fall forward. Then he collapses onto his knees and buries his face in his hands.

Watching him, I suddenly feel as if I'm eavesdropping, invading his privacy. I walk back to the table, hoping Jacob will return. As I settle back into my seat, I notice his keys laying on the table. Now I know he will have to come back. My wait turns out to be shorter than I expect.

I hear the front door open and look up in anticipation, but instead of seeing Jacob turn the corner, I see the hostess step into the dining room and look around. Her eyes find me. She walks directly to the table, reaches across and picks up Jacob's keys without making eye contact with me, turns and walks back to the hostess station. Again I hear the door open and close. Then nothing. I stare at the archway leading to the foyer, waiting for my best friend to come back, but he's gone.

I throw a $100 bill on the table to cover our tab and run out the door. I look up Rhode Island Street. Nothing. I sprint to the corner of Richmond, hoping to catch a glimpse of Jacob, but again the sidewalk is empty. The sound of squealing tires fills the night as a car peels off a side street and heads north on Richmond. It's clear he isn't coming back.

I stand on the street corner in silence, running the conversation we just had through my head, letting it replay word for word. Is there another way I could have presented this? What have I done? Now I am the one running his fingers through his hair. Should I chase him or just let him go? With another reception awaiting me at church, a chase is impossible.

The idea of leaving Buffalo on an unknown mission is hard enough, but doing so without Jacob's blessing fills me with doubt and dread. He has become such an important part of my life. I hate this feeling of knowing I have let him down so completely.

I climb into the Jeep and try to gather my thoughts. I don't feel I have the right to quit after having been saved from a certain death. I still have to leave in the morning, but much of my certainty has been torn away by Jacob's irate departure.

I pull out onto Rhode Island from the parking lot and drive straight to church. After what I've just been through with Jacob, the party will be anti-climactic.

The party guests include family, friends and other members of the church community. Of the roughly 90 invitations sent, about 70 said they were coming. Fewer than 20 are more than mere acquaintances. I make it a point to mingle as much as possible, saying thank you to everyone. Not surprisingly, the pastor feels the need to lead the group in prayer, thanking God for my continued recovery. If he only knew.

After spending time with nearly every guest, I begin pulling my immediate family aside, one at a time, to say my goodbyes. My plan is to leave early in the morning before anyone is up. I don't want to delay my morning departure with an elaborate breakfast and long farewells.

I start with Jeannie. "Hey, sis, thanks for the verbal kick in the butt you gave me. I'm glad you decided against the real butt kicking. I just want you to know how much I appreciate all you do to keep this family together – and for keeping me accountable on this journey of mine. I promise I will stay in touch and you have my permission to give me hell if I drop the ball."

She smiles and punches my arm much harder than necessary. "Like you had to ask. But that staying in touch had better include everyone. This trip you're taking is really affecting Dad. Don't cut him out. You need to give him a break."

"You're right, Jeannie. You have my word. But you know he doesn't make it easy."

"No, he doesn't, but neither do you."

Next comes Mom. She is busy being hostess, making sure everyone is comfortable and has what they need. When I tap her on the shoulder, she looks up at me searchingly, not wanting the night to end just yet. I give her a big hug as she turns.

"Look, Mom, you don't have to tell me to be sure to take care of myself," I assure her. "I have every intention of being cautious. Don't forget who my co-pilot is on this trip." She cries as we hug, making the embrace last as long as possible.

I find Hannah laughing, as usual, with three or four of our cousins. I take her hand and pull her out into the cool night. "You know I'm counting on you to keep this family smiling," I say as I put my arm around her. "And please know that no matter what happens, I'll be back."

"Promise?"

"You have my word," I reply. This is the most difficult good-bye. Hannah is a beam of light that illuminates everyone and everything around her. I almost wish I could take her with me. I hug her tightly, kiss the top of her head, and say, "I love you, Squirt." We walk arm and arm back into the building.

Once inside, I tap a spoon against a glass to get everyone's attention. "I don't know if I have had a chance to speak with every one of you here tonight. I know I've tried. I just want to thank all of you for coming and for your encouragement and prayers for me and my family during the difficult times. It feels good knowing my family can count on your support whenever they need it. Since I am planning on leaving early in the morning, I will say goodnight and goodbye. Thanks again for coming."

Aunt Lucy stands up. "Going? I didn't know you were leaving so soon. Where are you off to now?"

From the almost universal expressions of astonishment, I can tell that Mom and Dad haven't mentioned my journey to anyone. "Aunt Lucy, I'm sorry if you feel left out. I haven't shared my plans with anyone outside of my immediate family. I don't have a lot of details to talk about now, but I promise to fill you all in when I can share more. Let's just say I have a promise to keep. Good night all."

As I turn to leave, Dad steps up next to me and walks me towards the parking lot. "I guess you guys have got some 'splaining to do," I say, smiling apologetically.

He laughs. "Yeah, I guess I'll have my own speech to give when I get back inside. Don't worry about it.

"Listen, David. I just want you to know how proud I am – we are – of you. We're looking forward to hearing about your travels and what God will choose to do through you. Please keep in touch, for Mom's sake and the girls', too."

"Count on it, Dad."

"Here, I want you to take this," he says as he pulls his watch off his wrist. "It's always been good luck for me. I want you to keep it close by. Oh, I also put some money on your night stand just in case you need it, and I transferred my EZ pass reader to your car for the tolls."

"Dad, you didn't have to do all that," I protest. "You know Jacob was paying me more than tips, right? But thanks." There are a hundred other things I want to say, but I can't find the words. With a quick hug for my father, I turn and head to my Jeep. I don't look back, but I know if I did, I would see a father's pride lighting up the church grounds.

My car is parked at the far end of the lot in the dark shadows of some tall trees. As I approach the car, I see what looks like a shadow on the driver's door. The indistinct image steps away from the car and into the light. The Hawaiian shirt is all I need to see.

"Do you know why I offered you a partnership in Embers II?" Jacob yells as he comes closer. "Trust, David, trust. I trusted you more than anyone I've ever worked with. I trusted you enough to bet it all on you." He sighs heavily, now just a few feet away.

"So I'm having a really hard time believing you would suddenly become untrustworthy, a liar. That means you truly are doing what you think you need to do." He sighs again and falls against the closest car.

"I don't understand it," he continues, "but for some crazy reason, I still believe in you, I still trust you, David. Go, then. Do what you think you need to do. I'll still move forward with the club. Lord knows, I don't need the extra work and might even have to miss a Bisons game or two. But I'll get through it. Once you get this promise out of your system, your spot and our agreement will be waiting for you."

I stare at him in disbelief. I can feel the tears welling up in my eyes and see the same in Jacob's. Neither of us speak, but much is said in our silence. It brings us to another hug. He pulls away. "Now get out of here before I change my mind."

I give him one last smile and place a hand on his shoulder. "Thanks for everything, Jacob. This time I really will keep in touch." I walk once more into the darkness without looking back.

I make it home in five minutes and am in bed shortly thereafter. Ten o'clock is a very early bed time for me, but the alarm is set for 5:00, and I want to be on the road by 5:30. Fortunately, sleep comes quickly.

As it turns out, the alarm isn't necessary. The birds are up and chirping by 4:30, loud enough to rouse me. I had packed the day before, and after grabbing a quick shower, I'm out the door.

It is still dark as I load my single bag into the Jeep and back out of the driveway. I figure I can make it to New York City in six hours by missing all the traffic. NYC seems like a logical starting point because it is relatively close and as good a choice as anywhere. If you're looking for lost sheep, what better place to find them than a fully stocked metropolis?

I ease onto the I-290, heading for the I-90. It's a straight shot to the city.

A half hour later, the sky begins to brighten and so does my mood. I still have no clear idea of how this is supposed to work. All I know is that I'm on a path. Despite everything I'm leaving behind, the road suddenly feels like home.

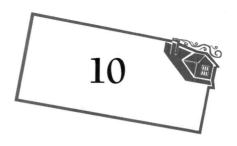

10

A First Encounter

Iᴛ's ᴀ ᴘᴇʀꜰᴇᴄᴛ ᴅᴀʏ ꜰᴏʀ a grand driving tour of New York State. I opt to drive in silence, leaving my iPod off so I can be alone with my thoughts. I have six long hours of peace and quiet ahead of me. I've always enjoyed the Thruway, the way it stays away from communities big and small, moving instead through the peaceful countryside. I spent many childhood Sundays on this highway en route to a visit with my grandparents in Rochester. But this trip has far greater meaning for me.

The quiet allows me to absorb the panoramic view. The sun is just coming up directly in front of me, and traffic is still sparse enough that I am making good time.

The highway gets busier as I move through Rochester, commuters mostly. The speed limit is a constant 65, and while I would normally push it a bit, I am in no hurry this morning. The mile markers move past my window like a metronome pounding out a rhythm. I am reminded of my trip back from Nashville, leaving my musical dreams behind. This time, my dreams lie ahead of me and I am excited at the prospect of being guided along what is still an invisible path.

As I approach the Syracuse exit, I decide to take a shortcut. I ease off the I-90 and on to I-81, taking me down through Binghamton and on to Scranton, Pennsylvania. This is clearly a different interstate highway. The pavement becomes bumpier, winding south through rolling hills. A fog rises out of the valleys, creating the illusion of flying over the land instead of driving across it. Three hours after leaving home, I pass through Binghamton and into Pennsylvania, where I make my first stop for gas. I'm at just about the halfway point to New York City, and the closer I get, the more excited I become.

As I approach Scranton, I turn onto I-380 toward the Pocono Mountains. At the Delaware Water Gap it will join the I-80 and take me into New Jersey. This is breathtaking scenery, the best so far. Towering hills rise straight up from the shoulder of the road, covered with a deep green spring carpet. The sky darkens as the fog thickens into clouds

The I-80 opens up into a flat, eight-lane raceway where cars speed along at any pace they choose. I continue to stay close to the speed limit, which leaves me feeling as though I am practically standing still. It's mid-morning, so rush hour traffic should be loosening up, yet the closer I get to the city, the more congested the road becomes. As I always do when I get close to Manhattan, I look off to the right, hoping to catch a glimpse of the Big Apple skyline. It has been so long since I've been in New York. I feel that my first glimpse of the Empire State Building will signal the beginning of my assigned journey.

I follow the signs to the George Washington Bridge, where traffic comes to a standstill. Inching my way to the right, I find the ramp to the Henry Hudson Highway and take advantage of it. Now I resort to instinct. I knew my destination was New York City, but now that I am here, I have no clue where to begin.

After hours in the driver's seat, my body is demanding to be stretched, so I look for a place to park and move around.

It's nearly 11:00 by the time I find a spot. I pull over on West 81st Street near the Museum of Natural History, about a block from Central Park. As soon as I get out of the car, I turn into the typical tourist, awed by the city's immensity. I head to the park to get a better feel for my surroundings. I walk along the museum fence until I reach Central Park West and turn right. As I round the corner, I can see the main steps to the museum. On the sidewalk in front of the steps is a coffee vendor, his large striped umbrella open and fluttering in the soft breeze. His sign advertises a wide variety of coffees and espresso, and I decide that a cup of coffee on my stroll would be perfect. I've heard the stories about the coldness of New Yorkers, especially in Manhattan, along with warnings about not making eye contact, so I don't expect a warm response, but this barista couldn't be friendlier.

I find myself hitting it off with the older gentleman. He tells me his name is Howard, that he's a former government worker who has chosen this cart as his retirement project.

"I work when I feel like it and when the weather is agreeable, or when my wife has had enough of me and wants me out from underfoot," he laughs. "The money isn't great, but I like the fresh air and the people."

After a bit of back and forth, Howard comments, "You know, David, you remind me a great deal of my son, Kevin. You guys are about the same height and weight. Probably close to the same age, too."

I watch the light fade from Howard's eyes.

"I haven't seen or heard from him in nearly two years," admits Howard. "He fancied himself a country western singer, wrote all his own stuff. Kevin took off for Nashville, and that's the last I heard from him."

My jaw drops. Hardly eight hours into my mysterious journey, and while grabbing a cup of coffee, the first person I talk to recites my story to me. It can't be an accident. Is this God's messenger's odd way of creating a believer?

Howard pauses and shakes his head. "I gotta admit, half the reason I got this cart was in the hope that someday I'd see Kevin in the crowd of faces that flows past me each day. He'd just walk up to my cart and quietly order a coffee."

"Don't give up hope, Howard. You never know when your son's dreams will change and bring him home," I offer.

Suddenly, Howard is quiet. His eyes stare past me but seemingly see nothing. He turns on his heel, walks away from the cart and sits on the museum steps.

I want to tell Howard just how much Kevin and I are alike, and not just physically, but the timing seems all wrong and I'm still not sure what my mission is meant to be. Instead, I slowly walk away, glancing back over my shoulder from time to time until I can no longer see Howard.

I keep on walking across Central Park West and onto a path that leads into the park. I am still trying to process Howard's story about Kevin. What are the odds of running into someone with a son living a life parallel to mine?

I walk along in a daze, lost in Howard's story and still amazed at the city surrounding me like prison walls. I gawk at buildings and signs, looking everywhere except where my feet are taking me. I step off the path and stumble onto a road that cuts through the park, right into the path of an oncoming bicyclist. I try to stop, but my momentum carries me directly into his front wheel. The rider flies across handle bars and lands awkwardly on the pavement. The impact spins me backwards onto the grass and I am now wearing the coffee I had intended to drink. I look back and see the rider lying on his back clutching his shoulder, wincing in obvious pain. I haul myself to my feet, swipe at the coffee soaking the front of my sweater, and move toward the downed bicyclist. He struggles to sit up, holding his arm close to his body and begins rocking back and forth in pain.

"Oh, man, are you OK?"

"I think I heard something snap," he grimaces. "What the heck is wrong with you?"

"I'm so sorry. I wasn't paying attention. I hope you can forgive me. I feel like such an idiot. Can I give you a hand? Do you want me to call an ambulance?"

"No, no ambulance" he answers quickly. "I can't really afford that right now. This is a fine welcome back to New York City. I think this place hates me." He tries desperately to support his arm, easing the pain.

"Well, how about I call you a cab to take you to the hospital? It's on me. I can even throw your bike into my car and meet you at the emergency room. It's the least I can do after what just happened."

I reach out to help him up but can't tell where to put my hands.

"And how do I know I'll ever see you or my bike again?" he asks as I help him to a nearby park bench. Logical question. This isn't Buffalo, it's Manhattan, where random acts of kindness are more the exception than the rule.

I reach down and take the watch my father had given me the night before and hand it to him. "Hang on to this as a sign of good faith. I'll get it back from you at the hospital." He reaches up with his working arm, nods, and tucks the watch away in his pocket.

It only takes a few minutes to flag down a taxi. I ease him into the back seat, give the driver enough money to take him to the nearest emergency room, along with a generous tip, and get directions to the hospital. Thankfully, the bike shows no serious damage, just a few nicks that may or may not be new. I climb on and ride it to my car. I load the bike into the back of my Jeep without any trouble.

I inch my way through the streets of Manhattan, following the cabby's directions, which are perfect. The main sign for Mount Sinai Hospital looms on my left, and a smaller one guides me to the Emergency entrance. I grab the last visitor parking space and hurry inside. I find the bicyclist in a wheelchair in the waiting room with his left arm strapped to his body. I slide into a chair beside him and extend my hand.

"I really feel horrible. My name is David, by the way." He looks at me and manages half a smile, but lets my offer of a handshake pass.

"You must not be from around here. Watch or no watch, I figured I'd never see you or my bike again. I've been away from this city for almost three years, and this is not exactly how I expected my first week to end."

The pain in his arm seems to have eased, at least as long as he remains motionless. I smile as I search for a small-talk topic while we wait.

"So...three years, huh? What brought you back after all that time?"

He looks at me quietly for a moment, as if he's trying to decide whether to share some secret with me. I break the silence.

"Look, if you're not up for talking, I understand. I'm not prying. I just thought it would help pass the time"

"No, it's OK. I've just learned to be careful with strangers. I grew up here, but left to try my hand at fame and fortune."

I laugh. "That sounds familiar. What was your plan?"

"I thought I was a country western singer, so I left home and went to Nashville. I got close a few times, but in the end," his voice falters, "I guess a New Yorker just doesn't have enough country in his soul."

That eerie sensation I'd felt with Howard is returning. I take a quick look around the ER, to see if someone is watching me – or setting me up.

Just how many people wander off to Nashville anyway? Why would I keep stumbling onto this story? I want to keep him going to see just how fast fate is moving up on me.

"Was music always a thing for you?"

"Always," he said. "I started singing in the church choir when I was 12 and found I was really comfortable on stage. While others got nervous before each performance, it never bothered me. It felt like the most natural thing in the world – being on stage, I mean. Once I got into it, I realized I also had a talent for writing music. The praise and worship team at church even performed a couple of my songs."

He pauses and then continues. "Karyn distracted me, though. I'd been watching her at school for a while before I finally got up enough courage to talk to her. We hit it off quickly, but then we ran into a wall. We were compatible in almost all areas but one – church. Her family never went to church, and she just didn't get it. She became jealous of the church because she felt it took time away from us. It got to the point where I had to choose between my life at church and my relationship. I chose Karyn. Does any of this make any sense to you?"

As he shifts in the wheelchair, he winces again and reaches for his arm to support the weight.

I'm not sure whether he is asking because of the look on my face or because he's genuinely curious to know if I am still interested.

"Yeah, it makes perfect sense, actually. Please, keep going."

He seems encouraged and pushes on with his story. "I finally decided to try and make something out of my music. I missed performing at church, so I took to playing small clubs in the city to work on my act. But that life wore on me. My music was getting stale. But I guess it was really more than just my music.

"Living in New York, even my relationship with Karyn, had gotten old quickly. All that motivated me was my music, and I felt trapped in the wrong life. If I wanted to succeed, really succeed, I needed to focus solely on my career. I finally made the decision to head to Nashville and cut all ties with my family and friends. They would be nothing but a distraction. At least that's what I thought."

As the last words leave his lips, I jump up and find myself standing in front of his wheelchair looking down on him. This is just too weird. I spin around quickly, scanning the room. Everyone seems locked into their own world, not paying any attention to me at all, yet I swear I hear laughter. I look back down at the bicyclist, still in disbelief.

He doesn't seem to notice my gymnastics. A new round of pain is apparently making him uncomfortable. I ease back into my chair. This just can't be a fluke! Did God put this man on my path on purpose? Who's supposed to be helping whom on this journey? I drift back to a dark stage in Nashville, wondering if the man in front of me in the ER had ever been waiting in the wings as the next act. Had we passed each other on the streets of Nashville, guitars slung over our shoulders, perhaps nodding to each other? The thought makes me chuckle.

"Something about this funny?" he asks sarcastically.

His comment brings me back to the emergency room. "No, man, not funny at all. In fact, you have no idea how familiar all this sounds. Almost spooky."

"Why is that?"

"How about you go ahead and finish telling me your story before we move onto mine? You're not going to believe it when you hear mine anyway," I explain, still looking around the room for some sort of sign, some clue that this is all real. He looks at me again for a few seconds, nods, and picks up where he left off.

"Well, I struggled in Nashville for 18 months with no success – not even close. I was finally offered a regular gig at a small club in Tampa, so I took it. I got a one bedroom apartment near the beach, but was far from happy. On Christmas Eve, I found myself alone in my apartment with a scraggly fake Christmas tree on the kitchen table. Suddenly, the depression that had been dogging me, building for weeks, hit me hard. But still, I felt the urge to create a new song for the first time in months. Instead of a country western ballad, it was like the songs I used to sing at church. Once written, I couldn't get it out of my head. It was as though the church were calling me back. The song calmed me, brought me some sort of peace and a yearning to reconnect in some way. It took months for the message to sink in, but I finally decided to head back to New York.

"Now fast forward to today, when you decided to find out if I can fly," he says with a grin. "Funny. Coming home has not removed that song from my head. I still hear it constantly."

He looks up at me and sees my smile. "Sing it for me," I say.

"When?"

"Right now."

"Here?"

"Sure, why not? I know a thing or two about music. Maybe I can help you figure why this song has such a hold on you."

"What, are you crazy?" he says. "Right here and now, in a room full of strangers with no guitar and only one good arm. You want me to just stand up and sing. They'll ignore my arm and send me to the psych ward."

"Hey, do whatever you want," I reply. "You're the one complaining that this song is haunting you. Who knows how long we're going to be sitting here. I thought it might help break the monotony. Sing or don't sing. No one has a gun to your head. But what if I can help get you un-haunted? You say you're not nervous about singing in front of an audience. So why not? And who says you have to stand up?"

He shrugs his good shoulder, winces, and says, "OK, sure, why not."

He begins to sing, softly at first, but with a melody that soon fills the waiting room. Everything slows down and those in the room stop and turn to listen. No one moves; not a sound can be heard but the music that flows into the hearts of everyone in the room. Nurses line up at the counter, trying to find the source of the music. Newcomers look confused at first, but soon join the listeners. An ambulance crew, pushing an empty stretcher back to their rig, stops cold, fixated on the sounds that have taken over the room. As the song ends, I'm stunned. All eyes are on the man with the sling. A small smattering of applause starts with the nurses at their station and spreads across the waiting room. A few come over to pat the singer on the back and shake his good hand, thanking him for the song. The bicyclist is smiling broadly from the unexpected ovation. To be honest, I am feeling pretty proud myself.

A nurse comes around the counter and approaches us.

"Oh my God, that was beautiful. I hate to break up the concert, but we have a room ready for you."

She steps around the chair, unlocks the wheels and starts pushing him forward when a voice from the back of the waiting room calls out, "Wait!" A man in a blue suit with a red handkerchief tucked into his pocket steps forward and says, "That was the most beautiful song I have ever heard, and I've been producing music for 25 years."

He pulls a card from his pocket. "Take this. Call me first thing Monday morning. If I'm not available when you call, make an appointment to see me. I can't promise you anything, but in my opinion, that song is one you can build a career on."

The bicyclist stares in disbelief. All he can manage is a nod of his head confirming he'll call. A tear slowly rolls down his cheek.

"I'll wait for you and give you and your bike a ride home when you're done," I say softly.

He turns slowly to look at me. "You know, if you hadn't run into me, if you hadn't gotten me to sing my song, none of what just happened would have happened."

"Then I'm glad we ran into each other," I say as I smile at him. With that, he is rolled away.

The time passes quickly as a deep and abiding sense of peace pervades me. This was all destined to happen. My time in Nashville was supposed to mirror that of my new friend. What magic brought the shepherd and the lamb into the same framework? Is this how it is supposed to happen? It almost seems too easy.

The daydream is ended by a softly uttered hello. The wheelchair has returned with the same occupant, but he is wearing a new sling and a smile. "I had to promise all the nurses a copy of my first CD when it comes out," he announces.

"You'd better add my name to that list," I say as we laugh.

The nurse pushes the wheelchair to the door and we head out of the hospital. I take over the helm and push him to the parking lot. The broken collarbone makes it painful for him to fend for himself, so he gladly accepts my offer to take him home and get him settled.

I ease him into the passenger seat of the Jeep, and as we pull away from the hospital, I say, "This has definitely been a long day for you. You must be starving."

He reaches into his pocket and pulls out my dad's watch, passing it back to me. "To tell you the truth, I'm not that hungry, but I could use a cup of coffee. By the way, I never did introduce myself properly. My name is Kevin."

Kevin? Oh my God, Kevin! Why am I not surprised? My mind flashes back to the face of the coffee vendor I had met only a few hours earlier. The final piece of the puzzle snaps into place. "Coffee, eh? Well, Kevin, I think I know just the place."

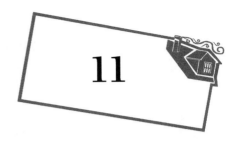

11

Defining Moments

IT'S BEEN MANY YEARS SINCE I've traveled the I-95 heading south through New Jersey, but toll booths every four or five miles remain a part of my memory. I have a whole new appreciation for the EZ Pass transponder that Dad had transferred to my car as his contribution to my adventure. Otherwise, I'd have spent half my time fishing for loose change instead of coasting through the toll booths. I am also thankful for the healthy nest egg I managed to accumulate while working for Jacob; it leaves me free of financial concerns as I travel.

I find a Super 8 Motel just off the Jersey Turnpike in Mount Laurel and decide I am due a warm bed. After settling in for the evening, I take advantage of the quiet night to fulfill my e-mail obligations. The very first one establishes a format I will use throughout my journey. Rather than writing individual notes, I begin journaling my experiences, sending out a single message to a group. The list includes Mom and Dad, Jeannie and Hannah and, of course, Jacob. After the events of the day, I also add Kevin.

I start my first missive by sharing the road trip between Buffalo and New York City. Then I talk about strolling through the Upper

West side, meeting Howard, and my collision with Kevin. I review the amazing similarities between Kevin's story and my own, trying my best to describe Kevin's song and its effect on the waiting room. I also tell everyone about the record producer and his plans for Kevin's future. I smile as I recount the instant bond Kevin and I formed and how talking with him made me feel as if I were speaking with myself.

The hardest part of the journey to write about is the reunion of Kevin and Howard. I describe how I pulled up along the curb in front of the Museum of Natural History, where Howard was busy cleaning the front of his cart, his back turned to the street. When I got out of my car and walked around the rear of the Jeep, the sound of the closing door caught Howard's attention. He turned as I approached the passenger door.

"Hey, you're back again," he yelled. "Was my coffee so good you had to come back for a second cup?"

"In fact, it was," I called back. "But I had to bring a friend to prove I wasn't exaggerating. He's a little banged up, so we'll be there as soon as I get him out of the car."

I describe as best as I can the scene of Howard watching me as the passenger door slowly opened. How I bent over and reached into the car to give Kevin my arm. As his head emerged, Howard dropped his bottle of cleaner and roll of paper towels and gasped. I couldn't accurately describe the look on Howard's face as he ran to the curb and took my burden into his own arms.

"Dad, the arm, watch the arm!" Kevin moaned. Howard could find no words as his tears soaked his son's sling.

"It's OK, Dad. I'm home, I'm home," said Kevin as he tried awkwardly to pat his father on the back. "And I'm here to stay. Jeez, Dad, go easy. That collarbone's already been broken once today." There was no more conversation between the two, only an embrace that wouldn't end.

I pulled Kevin's bike out of the back of the Jeep and rolled it up against the coffee cart. I hung the small bag, containing Kevin's medication, hospital instructions and a certain music executive's card, over the handle bars and walked quietly back to my car. I glanced back one last time to see a small crowd gathering around the still-embracing father and son.

I end my report home with me pulling the Jeep away from the curb, feeling a warmth that I had never before experienced envelop me.

I leave so much of what I lived this day out of my nascent journal. I am finding it difficult to describe the feelings that had come over me, how I felt about all that had happened. Other than stepping blindly off a curb, I hadn't taken any action to change someone's life. I didn't make anyone do anything. I didn't even know what was happening when it was happening. The only way to describe my role is as a catalyst that brings about change. Falling into Kevin's life – literally – and then allowing events to happen on their own. The simplicity of it boosts my confidence. Perhaps I really can do this. I find myself smiling as I hit send.

The next thing I know, it's morning. I wake feeling well rested. After showering and getting dressed, I make my way down to the lobby for the free continental breakfast, grabbing a bagel and pouring myself some coffee. I find a copy of *USA Today* on the counter and look at the front page in disbelief. There is a picture of Kevin and Howard on the front page above the fold with a caption that reads, "A Happy Reunion." I don't need to read the accompanying article; I lived it.

I refill my cup and head to the parking lot. I know I am close to Philadelphia, maybe less than 20 miles, but feel no draw to head in that direction. Instead, I get back on the Jersey Turnpike heading south. Before long, New Jersey is in my rear-view mirror and I am crossing into Delaware and then Maryland. I find myself heading into the heart of Baltimore.

Having grown up in and around Buffalo, I had always heard comparisons between Buffalo and Baltimore. Both are waterfront cities, but Buffalo had tried for years to develop its harbor, always managing to drop the ball. I'd lost count of how many times I had heard, "Why can't we do what Baltimore did?" Buffalo had even brought in the developer who created Baltimore's inner harbor, but the city couldn't close the deal. Now that I'm this close to Baltimore, I have to see what all the fuss is about.

It doesn't take long to find my way to the inner harbor, and it is everything it's cracked up to be. The atmosphere is carnival-like. Couples walking hand in hand, families with strollers and kids of all ages. Teenagers are sitting in circles on the grass talking and laughing, and musicians are trying desperately to make some extra money, playing for whoever will stop long enough to listen and toss a few coins in their guitar cases. The harbor itself hosts water vessels of all shapes and sizes, from jet skis to tall ships, party boats to work boats. I am duly impressed. I walk along the water's edge and sit on the breakwall with my feet hanging over the side. Suddenly, my journey takes on the air of a vacation. I take in my surroundings, feeling the hot sun beating down on my back. Everywhere I look, I see smiling faces reveling in the perfect summer-like day. The sound of children's laughter draws my attention to a boat in the harbor overflowing with a family celebration. Kids are climbing all over a huge sailboat, and of course, none of them are wearing life vests. I can't help but laugh as they scamper all over the boat, playing their own version of tag. The joy in their laughter is contagious. The kids have the deck of the boat to themselves, no adult in sight.

As I survey the harbor, I notice a man sitting on the breakwall, maybe 20 feet away from my perch. He looks out of place somehow. Maybe it's the camouflage pants bloused into his eight-inch boots. Or the haircut that clearly spells military. He has no hat or sunglasses, no cell phone hanging on his belt and, most noticeably, no smile. He is staring down into the dark water, motionless. He seems almost frozen in place.

I feel like I have to reach out to him. I get up and close the distance, sitting down a couple of yards away from him.

"Excuse me," I begin, "I hope I'm not bothering you but, are you OK?"

No reply.

"OK, so you don't want to talk to me. That's fine. If you change your mind, I'll be here for a while."

I sit silently for almost half an hour. Not a single word is uttered by my breakwall companion. I figure the silence will last for quite a while. I bring my foot up and set it on the concrete walkway, about to push myself up. As I start to move, the silence is broken.

"Ange," said the man.

"Excuse me?" I reply.

"Ange. My name is Ange, short for Angelo."

"Hey, Ange, I'm David." I smile at him as I reach to shake his hand. He takes it without hesitation.

"My offer still stands," I comment. "If you're looking to talk, I'm here to listen. No charge."

The last words bring a smile to Ange's face. "My dad used to have a restaurant. Each time he filled up a customer's cup of coffee, he'd always tell them, 'No charge.' It got to be his signature saying for everything. I hadn't thought about that for years."

I am encouraged by his opening remark and want to keep the conversation going. "Are you home on leave?"

"Nope, I just came back to Baltimore after three tours in Afghanistan," he says, glancing up at me. "Three long tours of heat, sand and eyes in the back of your head." Ange pauses for a moment, glancing back out across the water.

He brings his eyes back to mine and continues.

"A long time of never knowing who you can trust, since even the locals you had trained could turn on you and blow your brains out."

"Ange," I say as I reach my hand out for a second time, "thanks for your service. I really appreciate all you did over there. But I guess you get sick of hearing that."

"First time I've heard it since I got home," he replies, ignoring my hand.

I'm shocked. "You've got to be kidding!"

"You know what, David? I'm proud to have served my country. I've always considered myself a patriot. I remember nights, sleeping when you could, dreaming about coming home. Not coming home as a hero or to a parade, but at least coming home and being appreciated for my efforts.

"But I feel more like a forgotten man than a hero. For all I've been through, all the horrors I've seen, on both sides, I'm not even good enough to get hired for a minimum-wage job. Some hero, huh?"

I watch as this brave soldier's head dipped down again, staring hard into the water, eyeing his own reflection in the sunlit bay. I move closer and put my hand on his shoulder.

"Listen, Ange. You've come home to tough economic times for everyone. Jobs just aren't out there right now for anyone. Even high school kids can't find work because all the jobs typically filled by teenagers are being taken by adults whose unemployment has run out. I know what you've been through is much tougher in so many ways than the economic hardships we face, but we all feel like we're fighting a war.

"What we need to do is to sit down and make a plan for you. First, we have to figure out what you're good at. I don't suppose there are many employment ads for heroes," I joke. "But maybe we can find a government agency that gives preference to vets. Then we just have to put together a solid resume."

"Hey man, what's all this 'we' stuff?" Ange asks. "You don't even know me."

"Yeah, so how many of the people you helped in Afghanistan did you know? Besides, when have I ever had the chance to have lunch with an honest to goodness hero?"

That brings a genuine smile to Ange's face. "Who said I'm having lunch with you – or that I'm even hungry?"

"That was me," I said as I smile back at him. "With all these people milling about, there must be some good places to eat around here."

"If you like a good hamburger, there's a Five Guys within walking distance," Ange says.

I can feel his mood lift and see his shoulders square, as if his load has been lightened. "They just opened a couple in Buffalo, where I'm from," I say. "But before we go, I'm letting you know this lunch is on me, as a thank you. Let's go, hero."

With that, we get up and start walking along the breakwall toward the sailboats anchored close by. We pass the boat where the kids are still running all over the hull. We move past the boats and turn up a walkway heading away from the bay. As we walk, I start to share my story. About my mission and what has brought me to the inner harbor. I haven't gotten far when a scream pierces the air and we hear the sound of something heavy hitting the water.

Ange and I turn toward the scream and see two boys looking over the rail of the sailboat we had just passed. The adults are still below, not responding to the scream of "Timmy! Someone help Timmy!"

Without hesitation, Ange sprints to the water's edge and dives into the bay. A small crowd gathers, watching the returning veteran surface with a struggling child in his arms. But it's hard to tell who is struggling more, the saver or the savee. Ange manages to get the child's hands onto the ladder hanging from the hull of the sailboat. Just then, one of the parents appears at the top of the rail and reaches down for the dripping Timmy, pulling him to safety. All eyes follow the child as he clambers on board and into the arms of his father. What no one notices is the hand of the soldier sliding off the bottom rung of the ladder.

Maybe it's the heavy clothing or the steel re-enforced boots. Maybe it's exhaustion from not being able to get a good night's sleep, or maybe Ange is just not a very good swimmer. The hand that slips off the rung doesn't come back.

Like the rest of the crowd, I am watching the scene on the boat play out: father gripping son and son holding on to a father. But I am thinking back to Kevin and Howard just 24 hours earlier, and the embrace they shared. Are embraces, connections, signs of returning to the path, to the flock?

A moment later, I look for my new friend at the bottom of the ladder only to find nothing but water.

"Oh, God, no!" I scream as I dive head first into the water. I dive below the ladder, searching frantically for a sign of Ange until my breath gives out. I come up for air, gasping, and when my lungs are full, I yell for help. Only then does the crowd's attention turn back to the water. I dive again and hear two more bodies hit the water to help me. The three of us search for any sign of Ange, but find none. I keep surfacing and diving until I am nearing exhaustion. I feel the hand of one of the other swimmers grab my arm, pulling me to the surface, and leading me to the ladder where Ange had taken his last breath.

I pull away, jerking my arm free and try to dive again, but this time four hands pull me back to the boat. Someone pulls me onto the boat, wrapping me in a towel.

The sailboat's owner, one of the swimmers, comes over to me. "This water is too deep, too cold, and too murky to find him now," he said. "And with the current moving back into the bay, there's no telling where he might be. I'm sorry, he's gone."

I am inconsolable. Not because Ange was a good friend; we had just met half an hour earlier. It isn't just because he was a good man, either. Good men die every day. I am devastated by his death because I feel it is my fault. If I am the catalyst that brought Kevin and Howard back together, am I also the instrument of Ange's demise? I am totally consumed by what ifs. What if I had headed to Philadelphia instead? What if I had just left Ange alone? Would he still be alive?

The harbor police come on board and question me about the sequence of events. I retell the story as best I can through tears that refuse to stop. I make sure to point out the bravery of a man who was clearly not comfortable in the water but who risked his life to save a little boy he didn't even know. Once the detective has all he needs, he tells me I'm free to go.

The owner of the boat also owns one of the hotels ringing the inner harbor and offers me a room for the night, no charge. Just like Ange's dad. I accept, knowing I'm in no condition to drive. Someone walks me back to shore and I toss the towel to him before turning away. I wander over to the breakwall and stand staring into the water for a moment, just as Ange was doing when I first saw him.

A news crew approaches and a petite blond woman wearing way too much makeup thrusts a microphone in my face.

"Excuse me sir, can you tell us what happened here?" she asks.

I look through her while I gather my thoughts.

"What happened here is that a man who spent three years of his life being a hero to strangers from another country just couldn't stop being a hero when he returned home," I finally say. "At least this time, he'll get the recognition he deserves, but never got for all the lives he had already saved. He didn't wear a cape or a mask or a belt full of gadgets, but he was as much a superhero as any we worship today. And I don't think Ange would have wanted to live his life in any other way."

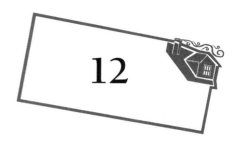

12

Circling the Wagons

I SIT ON A KING-SIZED bed in a room big enough for two. The television is off, my iPod is unplugged, and only one light is on in the bathroom. I am exhausted, propped against four of the pillows, staring out the window overlooking the harbor. All the confidence I had in this mission this morning has evaporated. What seemed easy yesterday feels nearly impossible today.

Whatever made me think I am the right person to pull this off? I ask myself. I keep replaying the image of a soldier sitting motionless on the breakwall near me.

If I'd just left him alone, he might still be alive. But then again, he probably would have jumped in after that boy whether I had spoken to him or not. So what have I accomplished? I wonder. What good am I doing? This is going to be a damned small flock at this rate.

Well, I have this room for the night. I might as well take advantage of it and try to get some sleep. Maybe in the morning I should just head home. At least I'm a fairly proficient bartender. This prophet stuff is way out of my league.

I walk into the bathroom and close the door behind me to get ready for bed. As I brush my teeth, I notice a bright light coming from the bedroom. I slowly open the door. All the lamps are on, as is the TV, but not tuned to any channel, just snow on the screen. I step into the room and there, standing by the sliding door, is my visitor from God.

"It's you again," I say.

"Yes, David, it is. I understand you are planning to return home."

"Yes, I am. I am not the guy for this job. I am supposed to help people find their paths. Since when does a path lead to the bottom of a harbor?"

The messenger steps into the room and pulls a chair from the desk. "Come, David. Please sit. There is something you need to see. Not everything is as it appears. This journey will not serve the Father, you or the sheep you seek unless you have some faith in your mission and yourself."

The television screen comes alive. I move to the chair and sit, keeping one eye on the young man in white. As I do, the screen of the TV lights up, showing an underwater scene. I can make out the bottom of a boat and two legs in the water alongside it. Suddenly the legs seem to drop and struggle, kicking in high boots and camouflaged cargo pants. The struggle is frantic at first, then slows to a drift. As the body turns, I can see Ange's face. His eyes are open, his face at peace. He slowly reaches a hand into a cargo pocket on his pants and pulls out a pistol. The screen zooms in on his hand as his fingers open, allowing the gun to fall away and sink to the bottom of the harbor. The image pans back to Ange's face, revealing a peaceful smile as he drifts into an eternal sleep. The screen goes black.

"What did I just see? Did Ange want to die? Is that why he had that gun?"

The messenger replies: "Ange had been struggling for a while with a decision to end his life on Earth. Prayers, counseling, all sorts of divine interventions failed to turn his heart. He was at the harbor today to end his life. When you arrived, he was minutes from shooting himself. You kept him engaged long enough to see the boy fall off the boat."

Although I am still saddened by the loss of a good man, I can feel the weight of responsibility lift. "So by allowing himself to die as he saved that little boy," I say, "Ange reaffirmed himself as a hero."

"Yes, David," said the messenger.

I begin to understand. "During that last, fleeting moment, he led a battle to save the locals from sure annihilation. Only instead of the sand of a desolate land, it was the waters of the Chesapeake Bay. Just as he tried to save a people who knew nothing but a life of conflict, he saved a little boy who had everything to live for. Ange was simply being a soldier again, a hero completing one last mission. But rather than his passing being recorded as a just one more death notice, he went out as front page news," I say.

I stare in disbelief at the dark television screen and turn to ask my visitor one last question. He is gone. Did I chase again as I did at the hospital? No. So what has changed? The small seed that was planted in my heart has begun to blossom. Its name is faith.

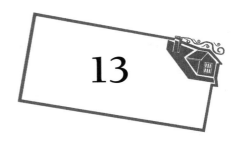

13

A Family Affair

IT'S ANOTHER UNSEASONABLY WARM AND humid May day in Washington. Good weather seems to be following me down the coast. I don't have a clue if this is where I am supposed to be, but it's been a long time since I visited the nation's capital. Why not take advantage of its proximity? It's less than an hour's drive from the Baltimore harbor to the beltway. My plan is to get on the road early to beat the dreaded city traffic. Not a chance! Once on the beltway, it takes me another 90 minutes to wind my way through bumper-to-bumper congestion.

I left Baltimore so early that I missed the free breakfast. Once I get within the D.C. city limits, I start looking for a diner to tame my growing hunger. It doesn't take me long to find one. I grab a booth alongside a window and order a coffee while I scan the menu.

The events of the previous day consume my thoughts. I'd lain awake most of the night, thinking about Ange. Might there have been any other solution to his issues short of death? Was there anything I could have done to save him? Close to dawn, I finally realized that my mission is not about changing the course of events.

What happened to Ange was supposed to happen. I was just inserted into his life to keep things on course. Two encounters, Kevin and Ange, so utterly different with dramatically different results. I have so much to learn about the people I meet, and even more to learn about myself.

I hear what sounds like sniffling coming from the booth in front of me. I peek over the top of my menu and see a young man, surely no older than 18, staring out the window, using his napkin as a tissue. His plate is empty and he has half a glass of orange juice next to it. His backpack is on the bench next to him and a menu is lying on the table across from him, giving me the impression that he is waiting for someone. He has short, cropped blonde hair, a thin face and the largest lump I have ever seen in the middle of his forehead. Other than the bump, he looks extremely fit and healthy.

The waitress delivers my coffee and I order a western omelet with bacon. Once she leaves, I take another look at the kid and figure I've nothing to lose. I slide across my booth, grab my coffee and sit down across from young man without an invitation.

"Sorry if I'm interrupting," I start, "but are you hurt?"

The young man immediately stiffens, embarrassed by his tears. "No, I'm OK. Why?"

"You sound upset and it looks as though you might be in some pain, too."

"Oh, this," he says pointing to his goose egg with a hand encased in a cast. "Nah, this is a couple of days old."

"How did you manage to get it? It's a doozey."

"I missed a lay-up in a basketball game before I left home."

We seem to be making progress so I decide to keep going. "What did you do, hit your head on the rim?" I joke.

That draws a smile. "No, I hit my head on a brick wall at the end of the court."

"So you lost your balance and fell into a brick wall?" I say somewhat incredulously.

"No again. I was so pissed about missing such an easy lay-up that I head-butted the wall."

"Seriously?"

"Yup, and then I was so pissed about hitting my head, I punched the same wall and broke a few knuckles. It wasn't a good night on or off the court," he says, his smile turning into a chuckle.

"Was this some sort of championship game?"

"Nah, just a pick-up game."

I stare at him in disbelief. What would possess someone to do that much damage to himself over a simple pick-up game? It certainly wasn't because of a missed lay-up. Part of me wants to keep asking and probing, but as soon as I think about getting more involved, Ange's face pops into my head. What if the conversation breaks down and I am faced with another life or death situation? Am I prepared for that? On the other hand, my whole reason for being on this road trip is to reach out to people. If I walk away from a kid hurting as much as this one is, I might as well just go home. Besides, there has to be a reason why every time I sit down with someone I end up looking heartbreak in the eye. I decide to stay right where I am.

"I know this is none of my business, especially since we haven't even introduced ourselves, but don't you think all that is a bit over the top for a missed shot?"

The young man snarls and slams his good hand against the table. "You're right," he agrees. "It isn't any of your business. I don't know who you are or why you invited yourself to my table." Then he takes a deep breath and slumps back against the booth. "I guess I've got a short fuse or something. I'm sorry"

"No, I'm the one who should be sorry," I say. "I didn't mean to pry. Let's start over. My name is David, and it wasn't my intention to upset you. I just thought I could be of some help. I'll head back to my own table and leave you alone."

"Hey dude, that's okay. You're welcome to stay if you want, at least until my old man gets here. But who knows when that'll be. I'm Terry."

The waitress appears with my food, refills my cup and then disappears. I reach over the bench seat to my booth to pick up my jacket, then resettle myself back at Terry's table.

"It's nice to meet you, Terry. Do you live in D.C.?"

"No. I came down to see Georgetown and meet the coaches to talk about coming here next year. I'm from a small town just outside of Cleveland."

"Hey, good for you! What sport do you play?"

"I was a three-sport, all-county guy in high school. I played soccer, basketball and baseball. I came down here to see the soccer coaches. They need a keeper and I think that's my best shot at getting a scholarship."

"Three-sport all-star, pretty impressive. You must be a big man on campus."

"You don't know the half of it. Three sports, National Honor Society, class president, homecoming king. You name it, I've done it," admits Terry, but without enthusiasm. "I don't mean to sound arrogant or anything. It's just the way it is. It's not all that hard in such a small school."

"No matter how you slice it, it's still pretty impressive. You must be excited at the prospect of attending a college like Georgetown. Is it your first choice?"

The smile quickly evaporates and apprehension returns. His intense stare bores a hole through my chest. His demeanor changes faster than a werewolf's at moonrise.

"No," he says coldly. "It's my old man's choice."

"You must have a backup plan, then. What's your second choice? What other schools are you interested in?"

"There is no second choice. This is the only school I applied to," he mutters without taking his eyes off the table.

"I don't get it. You don't seem very excited about Georgetown. Why is your dad so set on it?"

"Because it's the only college my dad applied to that rejected him, and he thinks it's the best school in the world. He told me I could apply to any schools I wanted to, but Georgetown is the only one he'd pay for. So unless I want a mountain of student loans, what choice do I have?"

"Won't he at least consider your other options?"

"I don't think the word 'option' is in my father's vocabulary," says Terry with a grimace. "My father is the mayor of the small town I'm from and a deacon in our church. He and my mom both teach at my high school. People don't normally tell Walter 'no.' It's his way or no way. I don't think I've ever really challenged him or put up a fight for anything. It's all sort of pointless."

"So I'm guessing sports are a way for you to blow off steam?"

"Why do you care?" he asks warily. "My world is what it is, and nothing's going to change that. Talking about it just makes it worse and gets me even angrier."

I push back in my seat, watching his emotions ebb and flow. I can tell he wants to talk, but it's also clear Terry has just about given up hope.

"Look, kid, I'm not here to drag anything out of you. If you don't want to talk, that's fine. I just know it helps me. But you're not me."

The distant look comes back into his eyes as he turns and looks out the window. I can still see anger bubbling under the surface. "Why don't you just go back to your own table? I deal with my life the way I deal with it and talking about it is not going to change anything."

"No problem. You do what you have to do," I say. I throw my coat back over the booth and start to slide off the bench.

"Dude, you want to know the truth? I hate baseball, I hate basketball and most of all I hate soccer. I play because my old man makes me play. He was a soccer player in high school but didn't start a single game in four years. He's been pushing sports on me for as long as I can remember. I'm so tired of going from season to season, practice to damned practice. It never ends."

"And you've never tried to stop, to stand up to him?"

"I've been doing what he tells me to do for, like, ever. I want his respect, but no matter what I do, I never get it. He has no idea who I am or what I want. I rebel, but not in a way he'll ever know. In fact…wait, you're not a cop or anything are you?"

"No, Terry, I'm not. If you want to get something off your chest, go for it."

"You gotta understand, no one knows all this about me. I'm not even sure why I'm telling you. I've just been hiding all this for so long."

I lean forward and lock my gaze with his. "Terry, if you want to unload, I'm here to listen. If not, I get it. It's your call. Just know I won't judge you either way. And maybe, just maybe, I can help somehow."

"I guess it can't hurt to try." He pauses and takes a deep breath.

"There's a side of my life my dad knows nothing about. And it's not like anything he would ever believe about me." Terry hesitates, looking out the window in hopes of finding the courage to keep talking. "I hang out with a bunch of guys he would not approve of. We drink, we smoke weed, hell, I've even done 'H.' I have my own street corner in downtown Cleveland where I deal and make more money than I ever have before. I go to school, to practice, breeze through my homework and then I'm off to meet my buddies. We party down by a creek, at a rock I've always considered to be my fortress. You know, like Superman. It's our party place. Sometimes we bring in a guest, any girl that wants to party with all of us. But even my girlfriend has no clue about this side of my life."

I slump back against the booth, staring hard at Terry as he glares out the window, tears returning to his eyes.

"So what you're telling me is you do everything you can to please your old man by day, and you're a partying, womanizing drug dealer by night." Terry just nods without taking his eyes off the window.

"Who are you, kid? Your two personas are so extreme. Which one is the real you? When you look in the mirror, who's looking back at you?"

"There are days when I really don't know," he mutters, slowly turning back to me, red eyes burning. "What I do know is that no one knows the real me, and the anger keeps growing inside of me and it's clawing to get out.

"Dad's Terry plays soccer every day; the real Terry hates soccer and would never go near a field again if he could avoid it. The Terry my buddies know listens to hip-hop music and dances all night long; the real Terry loves to listen to classical music but won't load it onto his iPhone for fear that his friends will see it. The all-night Terry parties with other girls; the real Terry is a one-woman man who eventually marries and raises a family. While my friends sit in their rooms playing video games, the real Terry reads the Bible.

"I hit my head against walls out of anger, not because of missed lay-ups," he continues. "Because I'm playing a game for my father and not for me, trying to be absolutely perfect at something I hate. I drink and party to douse the flame burning inside of me every day 'cuz the real me can't find its way out. I sell drugs so I can afford to party without asking for money from my mother. And none of these are the real me."

His tears are flowing more freely now. Terry looks out the window for the answers he so desperately needs. I want to reach across the table, grab him in a bear hug and hold on until his tears subside. Instead, I put my hand on his arm just to let him know I am still here.

The waitress returns and asks if I need any more coffee. "No, my coffee is good. Do you think you could find me a pen?"

She reaches into the pocket on her uniform and pulls out a short pencil. "Just leave it on the table when you go," she says as she turns back to the counter.

I pull a napkin from its dispenser and start to write. "Listen, Terry, I don't pretend to have all the answers, but you have to come to grips with who you are. And once you know, you have to start making decisions that are in your best interest, not your fathers' and not your friends'. Until you know who you are, really are, you can't make those decisions. I'm writing down my cell number for you. I want to stay in touch with you. Even if you only need someone to bounce some choices off of, I want you to call. This isn't your father's life, it's yours. Will I hear from you?"

Terry turns away from the window and looks down at the napkin on the table. He turns it around and reads the number. He carefully folds it and tucks it into his wallet. "Yeah," he replies, "I think you probably will. Thanks." He looks back out the window, his eyes overflowing with sadness.

"Terrence?"

The young man glances up, startled. Standing next to our table is a well-dressed, middle-aged man. Somehow, hearing Terry's story made me expect a hulking brute with a commanding presence. Instead, I am looking at a five-foot-five, 140 pound lightweight. His two-piece suit is perfectly tailored and not a hair is out of place. Certainly not the kind of man I would expect people would have a hard time saying no to.

I stand up from the booth and reach out my hand to introduce myself. "Hi, I'm David. I'm afraid I've taken your seat. I was just getting to know your son. Actually, I've heard quite a bit about you, too." That gives rise to apprehensive looks from both father and son.

"Well, David, thanks for filling in for me until I could get here." He turns his back and pushes past me to get into the booth. "Don't you want to take your food with you?" he says matter-of-factly over his shoulder.

I feel like a little kid who has just been dismissed. "Turns out I'm a lot less hungry than I thought. Nice meeting you both." As I turn to walk away, I hear Terry's dad take over the conversation.

"Well, young man, I just came from the office of the Director of Admissions and it looks like we're all set. By the first week in August, we'll be back down here for the first day of training camp, with coaches looking at us as the starting keeper as a freshman."

Us? I freeze. I can't believe this man just sat down across from his own son without even acknowledging his still-wet cheeks and swollen eyes. He doesn't notice or care that his boy is still staring out the window, refusing to make eye contact with his emotional jailer. I spin around and move back to the booth, standing at the end of their table.

"Did you forget something?" Terry's dad asks, clearly annoyed.

"I did, actually. I forgot to introduce someone, sir. I'd like you to meet my friend Terry. And Terry, I would like you to meet – um – what's your name, sir?"

"Walter," he responds coldly.

"And Terry," I continue, "I would like you to meet Walter."

Walter slowly turns his perfectly coiffed head toward me and looks up. "Once again," he starts coldly, "thank you for keeping my son company in my absence. But we have a lot to talk about, so if you don't mind." He turns away, dismissing me again. "I don't need an introduction to my own son."

I am not about to be dismissed again. "I'm not so sure about that, Walter. In fact, I don't think you have the vaguest idea who that kid across the table from you is."

Walter turns sharply toward me. "Who are you to tell me who I know and who I don't know?" His face is growing redder by the second. "That's my son you're talking about, and I have been raising him for the last 18 years."

"Funny thing, Walt. I think you have been using him more than raising him. I'm a bartender - a pretty good one. One skill I've mastered is getting to know people very quickly. You know what I see in you? I see a perfectionist. The perfect suit, the perfect haircut, the perfect town, school and church leader. A man who hates to make mistakes. You hate to make mistakes so much that you're using your son to correct all your past shortcomings. You're rebuilding bridges that you couldn't cross and living vicariously through this kid to make yourself happy. And you're doing it without any regard for how Terry wants to live his life."

Walter's face has bypassed red and is racing toward purple. "How dare you," he growls. "Just who do you think you are?" He starts to slide out of the booth, fists clenched. "I have a good mind to…"

"SIT DOWN," I boom, nearly making the walls shake, with a voice I never even knew I owned. Every face in the diner turns to watch. Even the cook comes out of the kitchen. He has a skillet in his hand, just in case.

Walter freezes. It's as though the sound waves from two words have physically pushed him backwards into the booth. Terry's gaze comes off the trees and fixes directly on his father.

"You are going to let me finish," I announce. I am towering over the table and over the little man who has suddenly been brought down to size. "Mister, you walked into this restaurant and started telling your son how he was going to spend the next four years of his life without even noticing his lack of interest. Did you actually think those were tears of joy streaming down his face? You have him going to Georgetown just to fix that little pothole in your life, that one rejection that made you less than perfect."

"That's nonsense," Walter sputters, trying to sit taller in his seat. "Terrence wants to go to Georgetown."

"Really?" I ask. "When did he say that? Did you even bother to ask him?"

"Of course I asked him."

"Then maybe we should ask him again. Terry," I say, locking onto his eyes, "do you want to go to Georgetown?"

Every face in the diner turns to Terry. This had ceased being a private conversation with my verbal earthquake and is now a main stage performance.

Walter looks at Terry with a wry smile on his face, expecting complete support from his son. Terry looks back at Walter. Fear starts to fill his face and he seems to be shrinking in his seat. I feel his eyes on me, looking for guidance, but mine are riveted on Walter. The round clock over the counter ticks off the seconds. The only other sounds are of a spoon clinking as an old man at the end of the counter slowly stirs his coffee and of the cook patting the skillet, hoping he gets to use it.

Terry suddenly sits up straighter. He looks sheepishly at his father and briefly clears his throat. Then he quietly says, "No, Dad, I don't."

A few small gasps fill the silence. The cook applauds against the skillet as he drifts back to the kitchen. The waitresses put their arms around each other's shoulders and smile as they watch.

Walter is stunned, speechless. But I'm not. "This is your chance, Terry. Tell him what you really want to do."

Terry takes another deep breath and looks directly at his father for the first time this morning. "Dad, my first choice – no, my first love - is the Oberlin Conservatory of Music. It's less than an hour from home and it's always been my dream school."

"But Terrence, they're only a Division III school. They can't even offer you a soccer scholarship."

"I know, Dad. And *if* I play it will be because I want to and not because I have to. But I can tell you now that I doubt I will ever want to."

"But, Terry, you love soccer."

"No, Dad, I don't. You do. And you weren't even very good at it. I played because you said I had to. I am not you. This is my life! Being an all-star is way more important to you than it ever was to me. Please let me live my own life, make my own mistakes. It's hard enough trying to deal with my own shortcomings without being responsible for yours, too."

The final words strike Walter like a slap across the face. His gaze drops to the tabletop.

I squat down next to the table, trying to catch Walter's eye. "You see, Walt, you can try reliving your life through your son's success at Georgetown, but what happens if in the process you lose your son? How do you fix that mistake? If that relationship slips away, you'll never be able to get it back again. Terry's standing at the edge of a cliff and, whether you realize it or not, he could disappear from your life at any moment, without warning, without a chance to say goodbye. Is Georgetown worth that risk?"

Walter slowly lifts his head and our eyes meet. He looks less sure of himself, but still defiant. He glances from me back to Terry, who is still gazing at him with apprehension. Terry obviously has never seen his father talked to like this and clearly doesn't know how to react.

Walter sits up straighter and puffs out his chest. "Let me tell you something – David, is it? I live my life for my children and

127

everything I do, every decision I make, is for them. I don't know what power you have over my son to make him say things he doesn't really mean, but I would ask you to leave us alone. We have a great deal to talk about and none of it is any of your business."

Terry gives me the blankest of looks, seemingly unsure of what to say. "Thanks for trying, David," is all he can muster.

"You know how you can thank me? Stay away from creeks and street corners." With that, I rise and step back from the table, turning to head for the exit. I look back as I place my hand on the door. What I see surprises me. Walter is sitting silently as Terry stares him down, talking passionately, and gesturing wildly with his hands. His last gesture is to point at me. It brings back many of the arguments my father and I had, with me trying to make a point and my father thinking he already knows the answer.

Suddenly it occurs to me that the theme of my mission is continuing to grow. Howard holding Kevin; a father holding a nearly drowned son; and now another father and son learning to follow different paths. Is this my calling? To repair a world where fatherhood is missing in so many families? Am I carrying a message from a loving Father who's reaching out to His children? Considering I had abandoned my own father for almost two years in pursuit of a career, wouldn't that make me an odd choice for such an assignment? Or maybe it makes me the perfect choice.

I lean my shoulder against the glass door, and as it opens, a voice calls from across the diner.

"David, wait!"

It's Walter, rushing toward me. He stops short at the door and awkwardly reaches out his hand. I grasp it and hold it for a moment.

"I know I was rude to you back there. I want to apologize," he whispers. "You may have opened a pair of old eyes that desperately needed opening. I don't know who you are or why you took the time to care, but you showed some courage."

I drop his hand and pull Walter into a hug. "Walt, I took the time to care because that's why we're all here. To take notice, to be concerned, to help each other, friends and strangers alike. I don't think that when our time on this earth is over, financial success, status, career or position will be recorded anywhere in heaven. Only how many lives we have touched in a positive way, how many people we have lifted up."

I start out the door again, but stop a second time to look back at Walter. "Walt, you've got a great kid back there with a world full of potential. He's not perfect and never will be, but neither are any of us. Give him a chance. Listen to him. You might be surprised at what you discover." I look back at Terry and gave him a wave. "And stop trying to be so perfect yourself." I reach out and muss Walter's hair, then push though the exit. I walk slowly to my waiting Jeep, looking back into the diner one last time. Beside the table where I had just been standing are a father and a son trying to remember how to hug in a relationship that had never seen more than a high five. I keep watching as they try to figure out which arm goes where, how to embrace intimacy where there had been none.

Strapped into my car, I take the cell phone off of my belt and look at my contacts. I bring up my father's number and move my thumb to the call button, but stop. It's easier to tell a son to open his heart to a father than to be that son. I need to fix this, but have no idea what to say that I haven't already said. I guess wanting to is a big step. But making a phone call just doesn't seem right. I hook it back on my belt.

For now, my path is away from home. The rest will have to wait.

14

The End of a Barrel

It HAS TURNED INTO ANOTHER beautiful day to live life as a tourist. Leaving Terry, Walter and the tiny diner behind, I spend the rest of the morning and early afternoon exploring the nation's capital. I love history, and a walking tour makes me feel as though I am somehow part of it. I begin with a stroll through the Smithsonian Institute castle. At first I feel like I could spend days here, but by mid-afternoon I get the feeling that I am neglecting something important and need to get back on the highway.

With a full tank of gas, I guide the Jeep onto the I-95 south off the beltway. Traffic is no better than it had been on the way into the capital, but once I am off the beltway, it opens up. I continue my new habit of not turning on the radio, my thoughts providing the entertainment instead. Unusual for someone for whom music used to be an all-consuming passion.

Each encounter of the journey so far plays over and over across the windshield. One moment I see Howard catching Kevin in his arms and the next I'm diving into the Chesapeake after Ange. I can feel the emotions of the smile exploding on Howard's face and suffer again through Ange's hand slipping off the bottom rung of the ladder. The emotional swings from elation to horror are disconcerting.

Themes of fathers and sons keep repeating as I drive on toward Richmond. My goal for the day is Savannah, some 600 miles and two tanks of gas away. It is what every southern city yearns to be, and its charm has always enticed me. I keep thinking of a quiet dinner and a comfortable bed with some time to send my journal e-mails.

Without my knowledge, both Jeannie and Hannah had begun posting my e-mails on a Facebook page. Each post garners more and more attention and "likes." My journey is attracting a legion of followers. Some are mapping my progress. I think my flock consists of the dozen or so people on my e-mail distribution list. In reality, hundreds are following wherever this shepherd ventures.

The interstate is taking me from Virginia into North Carolina and traffic is easing considerably. The sun is dipping toward the horizon now and I am beginning to feel the hours I have put on the road. Both hands are on the steering wheel, but I keep one eye on the road while the other takes stock of the odometer and the fuel gauge. I know I won't get out of North Carolina without stopping for gas.

I keep thinking about the big picture of my mission, what it all means and the ever-present question, "Why me?" After all, thousands of people die every day wanting one more chance. Why am I the one chosen to have my prayer answered? Is my journey unique or are there teams of shepherds crisscrossing the countryside, all over the world on similar missions? Each question leads to another and the more I think about it, the more questions I have. There is no way to find answers to all of them.

Even with the radio off, my ride is not devoid of outside entertainment. Text messages pile up as I drive. Mom asking if I am OK, Jeannie thanking me for the emails and for keeping in touch, Hannah with no specific message at all, just a steady stream of jokes ending in "lols." Jacob sends me pictures of the new bar as it is being built. Kevin sends a picture of a family reunion and thanks. The one text that really catches my attention is a picture of a college application to the Oberlin Conservatory of Music. No words accompany the picture, but it's clear who the message is from.

As the skies darken, I turn on the headlights. Cars and trucks flash by in both directions. I am reminded of a class project at Fredonia for a leadership course, a paper and a presentation comparing leadership to driving a car. I showed strong leaders as sitting tall behind the wheel with their best people riding shotgun, helping them navigate through life. These leaders praise their people, pushing and encouraging them to be successful. As leaders, they keep their eyes focused out the windshield, looking ahead to their goals and scanning for obstacles that could delay the journey or distract them from their goals. I confess that I thought of myself as that kind of leader.

Weak leaders, on the other hand, are rigid. They white-knuckle the steering wheel, afraid to give up control. Their staff is in the backseat, and the poor leaders never ask them for input on the journey, choosing instead to surround themselves with yes people who won't upset the ride. The weak leaders selfishly keep all the credit for themselves. Rather than focusing on the road ahead, they constantly look in the rearview mirror, watching for others who might be gaining on them to steal their job. They willingly sacrifice long-term goals in order to keep their leadership position just a little bit longer. Weak leaders put their own ambition ahead of the needs of the organization.

I was particularly proud of the "A" I got on that project, but I was even more pleased by the reaction from my classmates and professor. Our next class explored these two models of leadership and discussed them at length.

The fuel gauge is sliding toward "E." A sign announces, "Entering Lumberton, North Carolina." I take the North Roberts Road exit, hoping to find a gas station close by so I can get back on the road and find a comfy bed in Savannah. This means I have at least three more hours of driving ahead of me. A full tank of gas and some snacks should keep me alert.

A gas station appears right off the exit and I pull up to the first pump. I pop open the gas tank cover and slide in the nozzle. I insert my debit card and wait, but get no response. A second try – nothing. I can see the attendant at the cash register inside, but he is paying no attention to the pumps. Pushing the button on the speaker box hanging on a pole next to the pump does nothing to draw his attention. Locking the Jeep, I head inside.

The door squeaks loudly as I walk into the mostly deserted store. There are no customers, just the inattentive attendant.

"Do you think you could turn on pump two?" I ask impatiently.

The attendant stands behind the counter without moving, his hands pressed flat on the counter. His eyes lock on mine, but they are clearly filled with fear. I glance around the store again, but still see no one. Beads of sweat are easing down the young man's face.

"Look, mister, we're closing and the pumps ain't working," he says nervously. "There's another gas station about a mile down the road." He jerks his head in the general direction of the other gas station. Obviously, he's hoping I'll take the hint and leave.

But I don't take the bait. "Hey, man, is everything all right?" I sidle closer to the counter.

"Just get out of here!" he yells in a shrill voice. His shout slows my advance, but for only a moment. As I draw closer to the counter, some movement behind it catches my eye. A middle-aged white man in a black hoodie, baseball cap and jeans slowly rises. In his hands is a semi-automatic pointed at the back of the quaking attendant. The man moves around the counter so he can cover both the boy and his new customer.

"You just couldn't leave well enough alone, could ya?" the gunman barks. "You got a craving to be somebody's hero?"

"No, just an empty tank and an equally empty stomach. I'm not looking to be a hero or cause any trouble." I can see little but the barrel of the gun, now pointing directly at me.

"The only trouble is what you brought on yourself. Now get down on your knees and lock your hands behind your head."

I follow his instructions to the letter. "You do know this is extremely uncomfortable, right? Is this totally necessary? I'm not planning on giving you any trouble." I respond, glancing up at him.

When he doesn't say anything, I venture another question. "Do you mind if I ask why we are all gathered here?"

"Because I need money, and this young man here is going to empty his register into my bag, open the safe and empty that into my bag, too. Then the both of you are going to follow all of my directions exactly or you'll be dying here tonight. Understand?"

"Mister, I already told you, I don't have the combination to the safe, and we've been slow all night. There ain't a hundred dollars in that drawer."

The man shudders, then stiffens. He raises his arms and aims the gun at the center of the boy's chest. "Then tonight's gonna be much shorter than you planned. I suggest you find a way to fill that bag and fill it fast."

I slowly ease my arms lower. "I gotta tell you, buddy, you don't sound like any bad guy I've ever seen on TV. This robbery stuff seems way below you."

"What are you, a psychologist?" the gunman barks.

"Close. I'm a bartender. This is your first time isn't it?"

"Is it that obvious?" he asks quietly.

"Well, I wouldn't say you found your niche. Do you mind if I stand? This is killing my knees." The sweat is building on my forehead and starting to run from my raised arms.

"Go ahead, but don't be stupid. I do know how to use this thing."

I rise slowly, but keep my hands locked behind my head. The boy remains frozen in his spot with drops of sweat decorating the front of his worn uniform. His eyes keep darting out to the road, hoping for some intervention. Or maybe a miracle.

"So tell me, why are we really here?" I ask him. "What pushed you from being a pretty smart guy to being a pretty stupid one?" I cringe as the last words leave my lips, wishing I could reel them back in.

"You do know you just called the only guy in the room with a gun stupid?" snarls the robber as he swings his gun back to my chest.

"OK, so we're both stupid. But you being stupid means somebody's life is going to change dramatically tonight. Like somebody's going to be dead and that trumps stupid. Why are you in a life-changing mood?" I try desperately to keep my words slow and measured in an effort to remain calm and hide my mind-numbing fear.

He pauses for a moment, and I see his shoulders start to sag. "It's simple," he says. "I ran out of options. I got a wife and two kids and a house and a mortgage. I just lost a job that most people would tell you would be impossible to lose. The freezer is empty, but the kids gotta eat. So, like I said, no options."

"You've hit bottom?"

"You guessed it."

"What about your wife?" I ask. "Is this the bottom for her, too? Or will she hit bottom when her husband is in jail, talking to his court-appointed attorney through bars? Or maybe when the kids keep asking, 'Where's Daddy?'"

At the mention of his children, tears start down his cheeks. Small tremors start to appear in the hand holding the weapon. "What am I supposed to do? I promised my wife I'd always take care of her, no matter what. You tell me what to do, smart guy," he demands.

"I have no idea what you should do," I say honestly. "I don't know your world. I'm the stranger here. But I know what won't work, and this is definitely it. You don't want to kill anyone here tonight. The two of us have seen your face and heard your voice. Sooner or later, if you keep on this path, you're going to get caught. And what you consider bottom now will be far above where you'll be then. So you tell me what to do. And how, exactly, does one go about losing an un-lose-able job?"

"I worked for a big government agency, as if there's any other kind. I had three bosses, two who loved me, one who hated everything about me. I'm not even sure what I did to earn his hatred. But no matter how hard I worked, every promotion passed me by, every opportunity went to someone else. He openly ridiculed me and whenever something went wrong, he found a way to hang it on me."

His anger is building as he tells his story and I see the shaking in his hands intensify. Not generally a problem – unless one of those hands is holding a .40 caliber Smith & Wesson.

"So what happened?" I ask cautiously.

"I snapped," he says, almost too calmly. "I did exactly what he wanted me to do. I hit him and broke his friggin' nose. I can still see him sitting on the floor against the wall, smiling at me, blood pouring down his chin. He got me! Goddamn it, he got me. I gave him exactly what he wanted," he barks.

Pivoting, he points the gun back at the kid, arms stiff and shaking, tears still flowing. "Kid, you got to the count of three to fill that bag!"

"But, mister," the kid pleads.

"ONE!"

"I told you, there ain't enough money here to fill an envelope, let alone that bag."

"TWO!"

"Mister, please!" he begs.

Enough. I drop my arms and step between the gunman and the cashier.

"STOP!" I yell, with the same voice that had stopped Walter this morning. "So you screwed up and got yourself fired. Your lousy boss didn't do that. You did. And it's not this kid's fault that you chose to rob a place with no money. You did that, too." Despite the confidence in my voice, fear starts to overwhelm me. My vision narrows to a small tunnel with me at one end and the barrel of a gun at the other. The roar in my ears gets louder as my heart pounds and the blood rushes to my head. Two thoughts push out all others: how did I get into this? And how the hell do I get out of it? Just because God is watching over me doesn't mean that bullets are going to bounce off my chest.

"But if you really want to screw up," I somehow continue, "and you have to kill someone, then kill me and leave that kid alone. He didn't do anything to you. I'm the one who keeps calling you stupid. Leave him alone and kill me if you have to!"

Anger and revenge possess the man in the hoodie. He is pointing the gun straight at my heart. I see his finger tighten on the trigger and hear it click into place. Time freezes.

Had the gunman been in law enforcement, had he been familiar with the workings of an S&W .40 caliber pistol like my dad was, he would have understood what happened next. But he wasn't and he didn't. Instead of a loud bang at the click of the trigger, there is only a quiet "Pfft" followed by the sound of a brass casing being ejected, bouncing off the counter and falling onto the floor, seemingly in slow motion. Without enough powder in the round to push the bullet through the barrel, the squib load had lodged in the barrel.

The worst thing you can do after a squib load gets lodged is to squeeze off another round. The second bullet has nowhere to go. The gunman has no idea what kind of woe is about to ensue. He continues his string of bad luck and pulls the trigger again. The slide flies off the gun, splitting and bending the barrel with such force that the gun streaks up into the air and back, the gunman pretty much following the same trajectory.

The young attendant dives behind the counter. I remain standing, untouched. I carefully edge toward the shooter, propped up only by my growing faith. His hand is bleeding and his hoodie and cap are gone. He painfully lifts himself to his elbows, sobbing.

"Now this...this is bottom," I say as I look down at him. I reach down, pull him to his feet and haul him into my arms, holding him until his tears subside.

The young attendant is peeking over the counter, looking like a whack-a-mole. He pops up and reaches for the phone behind the register.

"What are you doing?" I ask him.

"Calling 911," the young man stutters.

"Why would you do that? Your money is still in your register, isn't it? And there is no hole in either me or you. As far as attempted burglary goes, it was a pretty lame attempt. Why not let me take care of our criminal here?"

"But this guy just had a gun in my ribs. If you hadn't walked in here, I might be dead right now!"

"But you're not dead. I'm just going to ask you to trust me on this. We don't need to get the police involved in this."

"That's OK with me, I guess. But I'm still closing for the night." As he speaks he steps around the counter. There is a large dark patch on the front of his jeans.

"Listen, before you close, would you let me fill up my tank?"

"Go ahead," he says, "I'll wait, but I'm turning out the lights."

Turning toward the door, I stop and look back at my attacker. "Come outside with me while I gas up. I didn't see another car here when I pulled in. You got wheels?"

"No, I only live about a mile up the road. I walked here."

"You are one moronic thief. Do you have any idea how easily you would have been caught? Why don't you let me give you a lift home before you get yourself hurt even worse?"

"Sure, why not? With my luck, I'd probably walk into a ditch anyway."

I fill the tank and head back to the store to pay for the gas. Before I can get there, the attendant comes out and locks the door.

"That tank's on me, mister," the attendant offers.

"Thanks, kid." I shake his hand, walk back to the Jeep and slide into the driver's seat. My passenger is already waiting for me. I reach my hand out to him. "My name's David."

He takes my hand. "I'm Craig."

After some quick directions, I pull back onto North Roberts. As I drive, I cast about for words of wisdom for Craig, but none come to mind.

It doesn't take very long to reach Craig's house. "This is it," he whispers.

I pull up in front of the house, not pulling into the driveway. A large picture window is brightly lit from within. I can see a young woman wrestling with what look to be a couple of very energetic youngsters. Tears are gathering in Craig's eyes again, and he is frozen in his seat.

"Craig, that's a picture worth fighting for," I say softly. "I get the pressure you're under. I do. You need to find a way to release it, but not the way you chose tonight. Anybody can handle life when the road is straight and smooth. But the real quality of your life is measured by how you handle the curves. It's not about how many times you get knocked down, but how many times you get back up. You ran into a lousy leader, a rearview mirror kind of guy."

"What do you mean, 'rearview mirror'?"

"A guy looking behind him for someone who might steal his job, instead of keeping his eyes on the windshield, looking ahead to his goals. You know, if I were you, I would find a good labor lawyer. Maybe you have a case against this guy. Maybe you can get your job back or get another position in a different government agency. You have nothing to lose by trying. But if you don't keep trying...well, just look in that window and see what you really stand a chance of losing."

Craig glances at the window again and sighs deeply. "Thank you, David. I appreciate all you did tonight. I don't know anyone else who would have stepped in like you did for a complete stranger. Man, I don't know where my head is at. I've got some serious thinking to do. But I like your ideas." With that, he steps out of the car and slowly walks up the driveway.

I watch him disappear into the garage and reappear in the picture window. Both boys jump into their father's arms at the same time. Craig's wife steps back and lets the wrestling resume two on one. The glow of family shimmers in the picture window. Craig captures both boys and holds them close. His wife moves in to make it a family hug. Craig looks through the window and nods at the headlights on the street.

Never had a rare squib load so affected the fate of a family. Just a few grains of gunpowder made the difference between disaster and a second chance for a family that so needed one. Those same few grains made the difference between the death of a messenger and a shepherd allowed to continue his journey with one more addition to his flock. It is a flock that I now know, more than ever, is not one of my own making.

My windshield leads the way.

15

The Messenger Receives

THE REMAINING THREE HOURS OF the trip to Savannah are uneventful, thankfully. I've had enough excitement for one day. The delay in Lumberton makes it impossible to reach Savannah in time for a quiet dinner. But the thought of a warm bed keeps me motivated during the final hour of the drive. I might even have enough energy left to fulfill my e-mail obligations tonight, as well.

I am still relying on my thoughts to keep me occupied on the drive, and with darkness obscuring any distractions, I am able to maintain a conversation with myself. I used to joke at the bar that, with the advent of Bluetooth ear pieces, people can now talk to themselves anywhere without anyone thinking they're crazy. Alone in the car, I don't even have to worry about being seen.

My encounter with Craig is definitely impacting my perspective. When I first left home, I thought I would be helping others. While this has turned out to be the case, I am beginning to realize that helping others is also helping me find out who I am. Not only does my heart warm with every encounter, my understanding of myself increases exponentially.

With Kevin, I was simply an agent of fate, causing an accident that led to the life-changing event of meeting a music industry executive. Yet I also brought Kevin back to his father, his family. With Ange, all I did was draw him into a conversation that seemed to give him a better understanding of himself and his role in life and society.

With Terry and Walter, I played a more active role, forcing Walter to face his impact on Terry's life. And my all too recent encounter with Craig had been the most active yet, confronting him under truly extreme conditions. My level of confidence seems to grow each day, a product of a clearer understanding of what it is I am capable of doing.

A lighted billboard catches my eye, directing me to a Hampton Inn off the Abercarn Expressway, just outside of Savannah. I check in and do my best to update family and friends on the events of the day, but my eyes keep closing as I type. The adrenaline rush from having a loaded gun fired at me at point blank range has totally sapped my energy. My eyes close for good before I push the send button.

My big breakfast plans become another continental breakfast and a perusal of *USA Today*. This is going to be my day to explore a city high on my must-see list. I check out of the hotel and drive toward the heart of the city, finding a parking place not far from Forsythe Park. The streets are wide, and the spreading trees drip with Spanish moss. I follow a map I'd picked up at the hotel on which I'd circled places of interest.

The city streets converge into squares, each with its own fountain or flower garden. Oglethorpe Square is an immediate favorite, with a statue and monument to its namesake, James Oglethorpe. I also manage to sneak onto a walking tour of Bonaventure Cemetery, which has been used as a backdrop in many movies. Why, oh why, didn't I bring my camera?

But the best is yet to come. I find my way to River Street, Savannah's waterfront. It runs along the shore of the Savannah River and offers night life for all ages. Two Mississippi River paddle boats ease by, serving as floating casinos. I am reminded of the French Quarter in New Orleans. The buildings are a little higher and the streets a little wider, but the same iconic wrought iron balconies hover over revelers below.

Strolling along the riverfront, I see a squad car pull up to the curb. The rear driver-side door opens and two officers struggle to lift a man off the sidewalk and into the back seat. It's clear even from this distance that the man isn't aware of what's happening. The whiskey bottles strewn on the sidewalk explain his condition. One officer gets in behind the wheel and drives away. The remaining officer brushes off his uniform and keeps walking his beat along the river, heading in my direction. As he draws near, I can see that he is definitely old enough to have paid his dues walking a beat and should have been in another position within his precinct by now, maybe even a higher rank than patrolman. I can just imagine what my father would have said about a cop like him.

As he comes closer, the officer touches the bill of his cap and nods in my direction. "Afternoon, sir," he says with a smile as he passes by.

I smile back at him. "Hello, officer. Nice job back there," I say pointing to the empty bottles.

He stops and turns back towards me. "Now, that's not an accent I hear around here very often. I'm guessing New York?"

I look at him in surprise. "Wow, good guess. What gave me away?"

"I think it was the way you said 'back'. Something in the 'a' sound. I'm guessing Western New York."

"That's amazing. Buffalo area, actually. How did you know?"

"My wife is from up that way, so I've spent some time there. It's not often you hear that down here, though," he says.

"Since we're chatting, I have a question for you. I don't mean to be nosy, but you don't look like a rookie. So how come you're still walking a beat?"

"To be honest, sir, I'm here by choice. I've had other jobs, been behind a desk, supervised shifts. But three years ago I volunteered to bust back to street patrol. I didn't become a cop to boss other cops, I did it to help people in need. I've never felt better on the job than when I'm walking a beat, so here I am, back where I belong. Why would you ask me that question?"

"Well, my dad's a cop. He's a captain back home in our local department. If he had seen an officer with as many years of service as I suspect you have walking a beat, he probably would have assumed that you screwed up somehow and had been put back on the streets."

He breaks into a loud guffaw. "You have no idea how many times I've heard that. The truth is, walking a beat makes me happy.

At the end of the day I go home a better father and a better husband. You tell me if the comments from folks like your dad are valid or not."

"No argument from me," I say. "I have a hard time remembering my dad being truly happy. He had a rough go of it on the job, and the man I knew, the man who was my hero, never came back. I wasn't always sure who this guy at the dinner table was. We recently went for more than two years without speaking. I miss the man my dad used to be."

The street cop is quiet as he studies me. He reaches up and lifts his cap back off his forehead. "So tell me something. When you say 'rough go,' what happened? And if now it's me being too nosey, just say so."

I laugh. "I'm usually the one asking the questions. No problem at all. Dad accidently killed a five-year-old girl with a stray shot during an armed robbery. He was never the same." I glance away and gaze up the Savannah River, my thoughts a thousand miles away.

The officer is just as quiet, but I can feel his eyes on me. He glances down at his watch and then back at me. "Listen, my shift ends in fifteen. You got any plans for dinner? Gimme a chance to get out of my uni and I'll meet you over there at the Boar's Head Tavern. Best restaurant on the river. What do you say? You ready for a real southern supper?"

He seems genuine, yet his offer surprises me. "Sure, why not? I'll grab a table and wait for you there." I walk along the shore toward the end of the dock. On the next block, I see the Boar's Head. I manage to snag the last small table before the dinner rush begins.

In a lot of ways, it reminds me of the Left Bank back in Buffalo. The same sort of muted atmosphere, with stone and brick walls, and it's just as busy with a similar young crowd. It seems as though the firehouse bell over the bar is ringing every minute or two.

As much as I'm enjoying the city, the Boar's Head and the upcoming meal with my foot patrol friend, questions about my journey start nagging me again.

I left Buffalo feeling like a very small piece in a huge puzzle, believing I was meeting an obligation, keeping a promise, maybe even answering a calling. But as my confidence grows and my role in each adventure becomes more critical, I have a growing sense that I'm finding my own path. The picture my father tried to paint for me years ago comes to mind. I had hoped to find my path with Jacob, but never did. Now, on this journey, I am finally feeling a sense of peace, recognizing that I am becoming the person I have always wanted to be. Lifting others up is one thing, but being front and center in one life-changing event after another is intoxicating. Music had not even come close to making me feel this way. Even on the best of days, I have never felt so complete.

"Hey, there!" The beat cop is standing alongside the table looking down at me, his hand extended. "My name is Eamon."

I stand up to take his hand. "David here. I saved you a chair." We sit down and small talk our way through ordering dinner. He tells me about finding his way down to Savannah and how much he loves the city. He speaks about family, the weather, and the drunk he scooped off the street just an hour earlier. I reciprocate with stories about Buffalo and working for Jacob, my family and bits and pieces of my journey so far. I still don't feel comfortable telling people I meet the reason for my trip.

As the meal wears on, my curiosity about what had prompted his invitation gets the better of me.

"You can't make much money in your job if you buy dinner for every tourist who says hello to you on your beat," I joke.

"I can't say this is a regular occurrence," Eamon admits. "In fact, I've never done this before."

"Then why today, why me?" I ask.

"I'm not really sure, except I feel the need to share something with you. You told me earlier about your dad changing, not being the man you remembered. Before the shooting, was he your hero?"

"Seriously? He was my best friend, the central person in my life. It was like his world revolved around me. Even my sisters were jealous of the relationship I had with my dad."

"And since the shooting?" Eamon asked.

"Like I said, he's a different person, cold, distant. I feel like I've lost my best friend. And what's worse, I don't feel like I'm worth his time. But you know what bothers me the most?"

Eamon shakes his head. "No, what?"

"I got replaced by religion. It's as if God became his crutch, and he can't get through anything without a prayer. How weak is that?" I ask Eamon, vacillating between anger and sadness.

We are both silent for several moments while we clean our plates. Finally, Eamon breaks the quiet. "David, do you believe in coincidence?"

"No, I don't," I reply

"Neither do I. I believe there's a reason we crossed paths today. Maybe you just need to hear from someone who understands what you've been through. I'm not a preacher, or much of a public speaker, but I think have something to share with you, if you're willing to listen."

"Go ahead, Eamon. Fire away!" I lean back in my chair as I watch Eamon's mood darken.

"I have known cops, good cops, who have been through situations like your dad experienced. They feel deserted, abandoned by what their life was before the incident. They can't get through a day without a healthy dose of remorse. Many of them, in fact most of them, found a crutch to get them through it. Some climbed into a bottle while others chased a line of coke. But the pain of taking an innocent life was so intense; they couldn't cope on their own. Maybe your dad turned to God, but what were the alternatives? He chose a path that allows him to continue to provide for his family, put food on the table, pay for your education and still be able to come home every night. He did it without drugs, without alcohol. I guarantee you, the man that sits at the dinner table with you spends most of his nights lying awake thinking about that little girl."

"I guess I never thought about it like that before, Eamon."

"David, if he was your hero before, he should be ten times your hero now. Able to leap tall buildings in a single bound. No matter what he went through, he never quit on you or your sisters, never made your mom a widow. Why do you think law enforcement officers have one of the highest suicide rates? If your dad got through all that by turning to God, you oughta get down on your knees and thank God for making that happen. And if you don't think your father's guilt is magnified by losing his only son's respect, then you're not paying much attention to life at all."

I feel like I was just hit by a truck all over again. I feel foolish, immature and hugely embarrassed. I don't know what to say, how to respond. I know he's absolutely right. I'd always considered myself an understanding person, but clearly I have been blind to my father's needs. I never put myself in his shoes to try and understand how he might be feeling. Now, with Eamon's words, my eyes are open to Dad's world, making me ashamed of having added to his burden. I bury my head in my hands and cry, sobs shaking me from the depths of my soul. I feel Eamon's hand on my shoulder, and I can feel others in the room watching me. When I have no more tears to shed, I try to catch my breath, feeling totally drained.

I gather myself, dry my tears, and look up at Eamon. "How did you know?" I ask softly.

"Because years ago, I was one of those good cops."

"You shot someone?"

"No. It was a high speed car chase that went bad. I T-boned a car at an intersection, killing a mother and two young children."

"I'm so sorry. How did you cope?"

"Let's just say I didn't pray to God. I paid homage to a bottle of vodka. And before I knew it, I was on the verge of losing everything that was dear to me. Trust me, I was no hero, not like your dad."

"And how did you survive it all?"

"I was blessed to have a woman in my life who loved me when I was unlovable, a woman who overcame her fears and doubts to stand by me, stand by our love and commitment. She had every reason in the world to walk out on me and take our kids with her, but she didn't. I am so blessed, David. And yes, that's why I went back to walking a beat, to be the kind of husband she deserves. Believe me when I tell you, son, that there is nothing more precious than a woman that stands by you, not only watching you get better but actually nursing you back to health. I don't know how she did it."

"Eamon, I don't know how to thank you. I've been such a fool." Suddenly, I know exactly what I have to do. I have to get back on the road. More importantly, I have to head home. I need to share with my hero all I've learned on my journey, apologize to him. I can't wait to have that conversation. But it has to be done in person, so he can read my emotions and feel my love. This final father and son encounter will bring one last sheep into the flock and make my transition complete.

I signal to our waiter. "The least I can do is buy you dinner instead of you treating me, Eamon. I owe you so much more than that. I also have some amends to make. I hate to eat and run, but you lit a fire in me." The waiter brings the check and I settle the account.

We stand and hug and pat each other on the back like old friends. Eamon looks at me. "I hope you don't mind if I sit here and finish my coffee. But don't let me hold you up." We hug again and part.

As I move away from the table, I stop and turn back to Eamon, now back in his chair. "Tell me something. In your accident, were you seriously injured?"

"Oh yeah, critical condition. In fact, I almost died, spent ten days in the ICU," Eamon responds.

"And while you were in the ICU, did you pray to God to save you and make a promise to serve Him if He did?"

Eamon just smiled a slow, peaceful smile. "No David, I didn't."

"Why the smile?" I ask.

"Because there was a time when I reached the bottom of my bottle of vodka, when I found myself just as close to death as I had been in the ICU, when I did say that prayer and make that promise."

"And is that why you stopped me today?"

Eamon just looks up at me and smiles that same knowing smile. He picks up his coffee cup and takes a long sip. Finally, he looks back up at me and says, "Isn't someone waiting for you?"

That's as much of an answer as I am going to get, but it's plenty.

It's nearly six o'clock, leaving me several hours of daylight for driving. I feel surprisingly rested and am ready to get back on the road. I race back through town to the Jeep. I turn the key and grab my map to chart my return trip to Buffalo. It is nearly 900 miles away. I look up from my map, suddenly feeling watched. I glance in the rearview mirror. I seem to see my dad looking back at me, smiling. Next to him is the young messenger, looking a bit smug.

Although the passenger seat is empty, I feel another presence, similar to the one I felt in the ambulance after the accident. Nothing I can really describe, yet it feels very familiar, very warm and accepting. I close my eyes, bathing in the warmth. Suddenly, I hear a familiar voice calling out to me.

"Shepherd, you won't be needing that map, now or anytime in the future. You have found your path and a growing flock is ready to follow. I am pleased."

I open my eyes and smile, glancing quickly at the empty seat beside me. I fire up the engine and ease onto the city street, knowing I have not only found my path, but have attracted the best of Navigators.

My path is more defined than I ever thought possible.

16

The Winding Road

IT IS WELL AFTER NINE by the time I find my way back onto I-95, this time northbound. It is late to start a long trip, yet I am so excited to see my father, I can't wait until morning. After about an hour or so, I exit the I-26 before reaching Columbia. If I keep going without stopping, I could get home by mid-morning. But I decide to rest my eyes for a few minutes and pull off the road.

I glance at my cell phone and see that text messages are piling up again. The girls are flooding my inbox with a constant flow of texts and pictures. Both Jeannie and Hannah have replied to each of my journal e-mails telling me how proud they are of me and how they are keeping everyone up to date on my travels. Mom sends daily family updates. Jacob sent me a picture of himself catching a foul ball at the Bisons opener. Kevin sent me picture of himself standing in front of the music producer's office with his guitar slung over his good shoulder and a huge smile on his face. But the surprise in the pile is a text from Terry's dad telling me to check my e-mail.

I switch over to my e-mail inbox and find Walter's letter:

Dear David,

I wanted to take a few moments to thank you for taking the time to care about Terry and me. You woke me up to the possibility that I could lose my most prized relationship. I know our problems didn't occur overnight and they won't be fixed that quickly either. But I have no intention of walking this Earth without my son by my side. He is talking and I am listening, and that's a great start.

Of course I am disappointed that Terry won't be attending Georgetown, but I am pleased that Oberlin is so much closer to home. We will be able to spend more time together to rebuild our family bonds.

Once again, thank you, David. If your travels ever bring you close to Cleveland, Margie and I would love to have you to dinner so we can both show our appreciation in person.

Sincerely,
Walter

The road is too long and the night growing too dark to focus for too long on Walter's e-mail. I want to read it over and over, but instead put the phone back on my belt and pull back onto the highway. I am deeply touched. Cleveland might just have to be included in a future road trip.

Another hour passes and the exit for I-77 north approaches. I am still making good time, and I'm not feeling tired. I am crossing into North Carolina when midnight rolls around. Whenever my energy lags, I open a window or crank up the volume on the radio. While I am looking forward to getting home, I am worried about sitting down with Jacob.

I know my days as a bartender or club manager are over. There is no going back to that lifestyle for me. The path I am now on has no room for The Embers II. It's not about religion, but rather the depth of faith that has been enveloping me over the course of this journey. Although I'd never been good at memorizing Bible verses, I know that somewhere in the Good Book it says others will know you by the way you live your life. If I've been trusted by God to bring back lost sheep, then I must honor that trust by leading the life for which I've been chosen. As deeply convinced of this as I am, I have no idea how to explain it to Jacob.

With Charlotte in my rearview mirror, I am passing through the less-populated areas of North Carolina. I battle my heavy eyelids by pulling off onto the shoulder of the road and walking a few laps around the Jeep. Then I climb back behind the wheel and move on.

North Carolina soon gives way to Virginia. I am crawling up into the Shenandoah Mountains, approaching the town of Bastian, when I see a sign that reads, "Now crossing the Appalachian Trail." This brings a smile to my face as I remember an item on my bucket list: walk the Appalachian Trail end to end. But that is a journey of a different sort: more than 2,100 miles from Georgia to Maine. Someday, I think, I'll find the five months it will take to make that dream happen.

Virginia is behind me and I am now in West Virginia. The halfway point – Beckley – is still a ways ahead of me. The night is pitch black, illuminated only by the Jeep's headlights and those of passing vehicles. But as I come around a slow, winding curve, the clouds ahead glow orange. Then the trees rising along the slope of the highway take on the strange orange glow. Rounding a final curve, my eyes widen at the horrific sight in front of me and I jam my foot hard on the brakes.

The road is blanketed with broken glass. Part of the guardrail has been ripped from its moorings and is bent like a discarded holiday ribbon. Lying on its side is what appears to be a charter bus with part of the bent guardrail passing through its windows. The tires are still spinning, so the crash has just happened. Flames are streaking into the night from the rear engine compartment. Screams are coming from inside the bus and smoke is filling the cabin. I reach for my phone and punch in 911 to report the accident, leaving my phone connected and open on the seat of the car so it will be easy to locate. Instinct takes over as I race toward the glowing inferno.

The angle of the bus as it landed had pinned the exit door against the remaining guardrail. The collision has also popped open the luggage compartments, scattering bags all over the road. Approaching the bus, I see a broken window near the midpoint of the vehicle. I scramble up the side of the bus, reach up and pull myself along the chassis to push my head into the open window. Utter panic prevails. Many of the passengers, although able to move, seem paralyzed with fear. Most had probably been sleeping when the bus went off the road. Confused and blinded by smoke, they need to get out of that bus as quickly as possible. I swing my feet around and drop into the chaos below.

I realize that the window I'd just dropped through is the emergency exit. I climb onto the seat and brace my back, kicking the entire window from its frame. It breaks away and crashes down to the road.

I turn my attention to the passengers. The new voice that had served me so well with Walter and Craig booms through the cabin.

"Listen, everyone," I yell. "Move toward the sound of my voice, and I'll help you out of the bus. Move quickly, and once you get out, move as far away from the bus as possible. Hurry!"

The screaming and crying diminish and I hear some movement around me. Smoke and darkness reduce my vision to only a few feet. Suddenly, a hand grabs my leg. I reach down and pull up a teenage girl. I grab her around the waist and hoist her toward the opening. A big man pushes past me and pulls himself up through the window. Once out of the bus, instead of running, he turns and kneels down by the opening, balancing himself along the chassis.

"Pass 'em up to me, and I'll pull 'em through," he yells. "It's getting pretty bad out here. We don't have much time."

His silhouette provides little detail, but I can tell he is a large man with a football player's physique. Encouraged by his presence, I focus on the voices around me. I reach out through the smoke, trying to find passengers. The growing flames outside the bus provide more light inside. I grab everyone I can find and shove them to the waiting hands outside the window. Young children, older women and students come within reach, and I lead them to the bright light and fresh air outside this ticking time bomb of a vehicle.

The noise inside the bus quiets. No new hands come forward. I move away from the windows toward the back of the bus. As I move through the cabin, I stumble over three victims who are beyond saving. It appears the greatest damage was done by the guardrail as it speared the bus and then out again. A woman in a sari is lying in the aisle where the guard rail had dropped her. Several passengers must have climbed over her fallen body to freedom.

Satisfied the back of the bus is clear, I move forward in the cabin toward the driver, who is still strapped into his seat, seemingly untouched by the accident. It looks to me as though he might have died while driving, causing the bus to veer off the highway. To his right, an elderly couple is settled in the doorway well, slumped against the door. They left this world in each other's arms. I turn back toward the emergency exit, convinced that all who could be saved were already outside. As I scramble over the seat backs, I hear a soft whimpering from below my feet. I turn quickly and dig through a pile of carry-on bags. I find a young Asian mother, holding the hand of a small child and clutching an infant to her chest.

I throw the remaining bags over the seats to clear the area and reach down to ease the infant from the mother's arms.

"Let me take your baby to safety, then I'll come back for you." She doesn't appear to understand me. Either her injuries are too severe, or she doesn't understand English. She offers no resistance as I lift the child away. I climb back to the emergency exit, pushing the child into waiting hands. I glance at the back of the bus where the flames had now entered the interior of the cabin and seem to be growing rapidly. The heat pushes me away almost immediately as I head back toward the mother. I finally reach her and hold out my hand to the young child. She pulls back, not wanting to leave her mother.

"Come on, honey, come with me. Let me get you out, and I'll come back for Mommy."

She looks up at me and as our eyes meet, she releases her grip on her mother's hand. I pull her up and race back toward the growing flames. As she is pulled to safety, she looks back once more into the bus.

"MOMMY!" she wails.

"I got her, baby. You go ahead and I'll get her."

I jump back down one more time as the flames roar toward me. I throw myself over the seats to get to the waiting mother. The flames light up the young mother. Throwing off the last bags, I see her legs are trapped beneath the contorted seat, clearly pinned. I throw all my weight against the seat, but it won't budge. I prop my feet against the bottom of the seat and push hard, but there is no movement. I reach down under the seat and as I do, a hand grasps my sleeve.

"Go," she says weakly. She is staring at the reflection of flames over my head.

"I can't leave you here," I yell back.

She pulls me closer. "Go, please," she says again. "And sir, thank you for my babies." With that, her eyes flutter and her head drops to the side, her eyes fixed on the flames over my head. I feel for a pulse, but find none.

I climb back up, only to find the path back to the emergency exit blocked by flames. I climb forward toward the driver and release his seat belt, shoving his body into the well with the elderly couple. I tear open the driver's sliding window and push my head and shoulders up through the open window as my feet search for something to push against. Nothing but air.

"Here – grab my hand." It's the football player again, holding out a hand lacerated by broken glass and blistered from touching the metal chassis of the bus. The giant of a man pulls with all his strength and I pop out the window like a slice of toast from a toaster. We tumble down the side of the bus onto the pavement and race to the grassy hillside where the passengers are cowering. Halfway there, the forest lights up as the bus explodes, sending flames high above.

The impact of the explosion catapults me forward and I fly into the air again, this time landing on my back. When I open my eyes, thousands of sparks are floating upward, intermingling with the stars and a full moon, like a magic wand painting the vista. The moon is suddenly eclipsed by the mountain of a man as he once again offers me a hand.

Sirens fill the night as rescue crews arrive from Beckley. Firefighters move to extinguish the flames while the state police move survivors to higher ground. The EMTs circulate among the survivors, administering to those who need treatment and distributing blankets.

I rise and reach down to help the football player to his feet. "Do you think we got 'em all out?" he asks as he brushes himself off.

"All who were saveable. I counted seven who didn't make it, but there could have been more," I reply.

"I've never seen anything like this, and I thought I'd seen it all," the football player says.

"Thanks for saving my life," I say. "I didn't think I was going to get out that window and those flames were right at my toes. By the way, my name is David."

"Hey, no problem. But from what I just witnessed, I'm sure you would have done the same for me. In fact, if you hadn't come along, I don't think any of us would have snapped out of it in time. And I'm Jonathan."

I reach out to shake his hand, but Jonathan will settle for nothing less than a bear hug. Just then, an elderly man now huddling in a blanket calls weakly from the hillside.

"Who are you?" he asks.

Jonathan and I turn toward the voice. Jonathan replies first. "Who, me?"

"No, the shorter young man next to you. Who are you?"

"My name is David."

"OK, so that's your name. But who – or maybe what – are you?"

"I'm afraid I don't understand your question." At that moment, an emergency vehicle turns its lights on the survivors, flooding me in its full glow.

"Look at us," the old man says. "We're all wrapped in blankets, our hair singed, our skin bleeding and burned, soot and smudges all over our tattered clothes and body, like guests of honor at a pig roast. Now look at you. You jumped into a smoke-filled bus, climbed over seats and were chased by flames and there isn't a spot of soot on your face, nor any kind of injury. So tell us, who are you?"

Jonathan peers at me under the bright lights. "Man, he's right. You're spotless. I just went through what you did and look at me. I'm a mess."

I look down at my hands. They're right. Jonathan has severe cuts and burns all over, but I look like I never even went near the bus, aside from a bit of soot on my clothes. I look like I did when I stepped out of the Jeep. I think of the gun that had been pointed at my chest just 36 hours earlier. Yes, the gun misfired, but was it really an accident? Now this. Am I being protected in some way, being kept from harm? How could anyone move around in that bus and emerge uninjured?

Even if I'm ready to accept that I'm a messenger with divine guidance, how do I explain it to everyone here?

"So, tell us," the old man insists. "What just happened here?"

"Best I can tell, your driver died while driving, and the bus crashed. I came along at a moment when anyone with a conscience would have done exactly what I did. I pitched in and helped, along with Jonathan, to save as many people as possible from a potential catastrophe."

Jonathan barely lets me finish before he jumps in. "I can't say I've ever lived through a miracle before, but I've read about them and heard witness accounts of them. If you ask me, we've all seen one tonight. Fate took our bus off the road, but the hand of God swooped down and placed this angel in our midst to save us. If I had any doubts when we rolled off the side of that bus, looking at you now removes them. Talk all you want about it, but you'll never convince me that this is anything less than a miracle."

I look at Jonathan and back at the survivors and I shudder. It's not every day someone calls you an angel of God. I could argue against Jonathan's theory, but if I am wrong, it would be like denying

God. At the same time, how does one jump up and announce that he's on God's payroll?

The dilemma is solved by a soft voice. The little Asian girl pads up to me and turns her tear-stained face up at me. Still hiccoughing with sobs, she reaches out and closes my shirttail in her pudgy fist. At first I think she's going to wipe her eyes, so I reach down to help her. Then she smiles ever so softly and quietly offers her reply:

"Amen."

17

Last Legs

THE BATTERED PASSENGERS HUDDLE ALONG the roadside as they wait for another bus to take them to a shelter. A West Virginia state police cruiser is directing traffic around the accident scene, and investigators question the passengers, including Jonathan, about how the accident happened. They save me for last and for special treatment. I am escorted to an SUV, where I slide into the passenger seat. In the driver's seat is the lead accident investigator, a burly man with a thick walrus moustache.

I speak slowly and tell the story as I recall it, beginning with my arrival on the scene and ending with me and Jonathan rolling down the side of the bus after I popped out of the driver's window. I don't repeat the passengers' speculation on my role. Unfortunately, my near-spotless appearance does not escape the trained eye of the trooper.

"Well sir," he begins, "that was a mighty brave thing you did here tonight. And I have no reason to doubt your story, since everyone I've spoken to so far tells pretty much the same story you do. So you're sayin' you jumped into a burning bus, climbed over a bunch of seats, shoved a bunch of people through a window and then managed to save yourself by squeezing through a window, rolling on the ground and then running as the bus exploded behind you, knocking you to the ground again. Is that about right?"

"Yes, sir, sounds like you got it," I answer.

"Did you leave anything out?"

"No, officer, that's about it."

"Did you clean yourself up before we arrived on the scene?"

"No, sir."

"Then tell me, son, how do you explain the fact that without these people's eyewitness testimony, no one would be able to tell that you were in that bus for even a minute?"

"I lead a clean life?" I joked.

"I gotta tell you, young man, I would be careful about being a smartass with me when there are seven bodies not more than 100 feet away. So far tonight, everyone says you're a hero. That you came out of nowhere and served to keep the body count down. I have even listened to the 911 call you made and it is clearly you. The caller ID matches that phone lying back there in your Jeep. I got no reason at all to suspect you of a thing. Just don't start pissing me off, or I'll start doubting the obvious."

"I really am sorry, sir. I didn't mean any disrespect. It's just been a very long day. My condition has been pointed out to me and I can't explain it. I know it doesn't make a lot of sense. Not even to me."

"Apology accepted. I don't see any reason why I might need to talk to you again, but I have your cell number if I come up with any more questions. What are your plans now?"

"The way I'm feeling right now, I'm thinking about heading into Beckley, getting a room and sleeping for a while."

"Then here, let me give you a voucher for the Hampton Inn a few miles ahead. It's the least the state of West Virginia can do for you after what you've done here tonight." He pulls a form out of his briefcase and fills in the information off of my driver's license.

"Thank you, sir. I just did what I think anyone would have done. No more, no less. I will accept your hospitality, though, and thank you."

I shake the investigator's hand, slide out of the SUV and head back to the hillside. I say my goodbyes to the waiting travelers and turn to Jonathan, who envelops me in another massive bear hug. When I manage to break free, rib cage intact, I find the rest of the group lining up to exchange hugs as well. For some, including me, tears flow freely. We exchange e-mail addresses and promise that we really will keep in touch. With a list of names this long, perhaps I will try to use Facebook to keep in touch with them once I get home.

Although I might look as fresh as a daisy, I feel like I've put in one heck of a day. On the back side of another adrenaline rush, I am utterly exhausted. I shuffle back to the Jeep and the trooper directing traffic lifts the tape after getting the thumbs up from the lead investigator.

It is less than 30 minutes to Beckley and a waiting hotel room. The Hampton Inn is easy to find using the investigator's directions. The night manager isn't too thrilled at my late arrival. He is even more annoyed when I present the voucher from the state police instead of a credit card, meaning he has to do extra paperwork to process the voucher.

I briefly consider doing my nightly e-mail check, but there is no way my body will cooperate. I do not set an alarm, nor do I request a wakeup call. I decide to let nature determine my agenda. The sky is brightening as my head hits the pillow and within seconds, I am sound asleep. However, nightmarish scenes from the last few hours invade my slumber. The smoke and flames enveloping my body, every part of the bus I touch superheated by the inferno, screams of fear ripping through my head. I snap awake and into a sitting position, running from the approaching fire. The words "go" and "thank you" from a dying mother echo in my head. Though my sleep is long, it is far from restful.

It is long past the continental breakfast hours and even past lunch time when I finally wake. I jump out of bed and roar through a shower. With a reloaded backpack over my shoulder, I head for the door and go directly to the Jeep. Two pieces of paper are tucked under the wipers.

The first is a note from the lead investigator. He has completed his review of the events of the previous night and found the accident to be just that. The sudden death of the driver had caused the bus to veer off the road. He thanks me again for my cooperation and tells me I will probably not be hearing from him again. He thanks me on behalf of the state of West Virginia for stepping up when most men would not. I am touched by these last words, but more relieved that the accident is a closed case.

Opening the second note, I find the handwriting of a young child. It reads:

> *Dear Mister David,*
>
> *I hope you had a good night's sleep. Thank you for saving my life and my little brother's life, too. Thank you for trying so hard to save my mommy, too. We will miss her, but I know my daddy will take good care of us. Whenever I think of my mommy, I will think of you, too.*
>
> *Love,*
> *Melissa*

At the bottom of the letter is a heart drawn for me and a second note that reads:

> *Be well, my friend.*

It is signed, "Jonathan."

I turn my back to the Jeep and lean against the side. I ease down the driver's side door into a crouch and bury my head between my knees as tears began to fall.

I cry for the seven souls I wasn't able to save.

I cry for the 40 others I could.

I cry for a little girl who offers such pure hope despite her own loss.

And I cry with thankfulness for the opportunity to have been there for them.

A Bible verse comes to mind, the one about how a good shepherd would leave his entire flock to save just one lost lamb. That image is so clear to me now. Not only as the shepherd who saves, but also as the lamb that needs saving. My eyes have been opened to my path and to who I am and to the gifts with which I have been blessed.

With this thought, my tears begin to dry.

18

Burning Embers

THE HUM OF TIRES ON pavement is the only sound as my Jeep pulls onto I-79 north. I have about six hours of driving ahead of me before I get to Buffalo. The gas tank is now full and should last me all the way home.

The closer I get, the stronger the gravitational pull of home on my vehicle. I've always had a lead foot, but long trips seem to make it heavier, especially on the home stretch. During the Pittsburgh to Erie leg, I blow through not one, but two speed traps. Each time, I glance into my rearview mirror looking for flashing lights. Nothing. Not being stopped just serves to reinforce the growing belief that I enjoy some higher level of protection. It's comforting to feel like someone's watching out for me.

As the miles fly by, the image of Melissa's face is never far away. I keep seeing her mother urging me to leave the bus. In fact, every encounter I've experienced since leaving home seems to float just beneath my conscious mind, as though my brain is now a multiplex theater with ten screens playing simultaneously.

The Jeep edges onto the exit ramp, taking me from I-79 to I-90. Just 120 miles to Buffalo. The dashboard clock reads a tad shy of six o'clock. It's Friday night, putting Jacob at the helm of the Breakwall. If I stop there, I'll get home later than I want to. But I know I owe him the courtesy of delivering my bad news as soon as possible. It's not going to be easy to close out that portion of my life, but I hope Jacob will understand. He's been so good to me.

I pull off the Thruway at Silver Creek, just as I had done on my return from Nashville, and head toward the beach. I find a prime parking spot right across from the side deck. It's a hot summer evening, and even this early, I can tell it's going to be a big night for business. All the deck tables are occupied, as are the beachside chairs. Two volleyball games are underway and a couple more teams are warming up, waiting for games to end.

Weaving among the deck chairs, I squeeze past patrons too occupied to notice. Turning onto the main deck, I see the band setting up for the evening gig. Until they're ready, the sound system provides the tunes. Passing through the double doors, I pause a moment to let my eyes adjust. When they do, I find Jacob's throne at the end of the bar vacant. I move toward his stool to check the Bisons schedule hanging behind it. Sure enough, the Bisons are at home against the Lehigh Valley Iron Pigs. Not only is there a game, there's the Friday night bash with fireworks. Jacob won't be returning to the Breakwall for a while.

Frustrated at myself for not having called first, I kick the base of the nearest bar stool. The noise catches the bartender's attention.

"Hey there, pal. Go easy on the furniture," the bartender chides. I don't recognize him, but that doesn't surprise me, considering the usual rapid turnover of staff at a bar.

"Sorry about that," I reply. "I just stopped by to see Jacob and am ticked at myself for not having checked the Bisons schedule first." Just then, Janice, the head waitress, comes sailing around the corner of the bar.

"David, is that you?" she asks. "What are you doing here? Are you coming back to work?" She throws her arms around my neck and hugs me hard.

"No, Janice. I just stopped in to catch up with Jacob."

"Oh my God," the bartender blurts. "Is this *the* David, the world's best bartender that Jake never shuts up about?" Turning to me, he asks, "Are you the guy wandering the world who we've all been following on Facebook?"

In all the years I'd known him, I'd never called Jacob "Jake" and I was a little surprised and a bit perturbed to hear it from this guy.

"Well, I'm the David who's spent a few hours behind this bar," I say as I reach across the polished wood to shake his hand. "He really has you following me on Facebook?"

"Are you kidding?" he replies. "That's all he talks about. My name's Ethan. Why don't you grab a seat? Every once in a while, Jake will call to check up on us. If he does, I'll tell him you're here."

"Thanks, Ethan, I guess I will hang around for a bit."

I turned back to Janice. "When did Jacob start calling from a ball game? He never did that," I ask quietly.

"Ever since you left," Janice says as she pats me on the shoulder.

Ethan jumps back in. "What can I get you, David?"

"Just an iced tea, sweetened, please." I ease onto my regular stool right next to Jacob's throne and survey the kingdom. Nothing much has changed, except for a new picture behind the bar. It's of me and Jacob. It was taken when we announced the proposed Embers II. My survey is interrupted by a tall iced tea and a napkin. I look up to say thanks, but Ethan has already moved on to another customer at the far end of the bar.

I study the interaction between bartender and customer. Ethan is waiting for a response, but his customer never looks up. Ethan picks up the empty glass and wipes down the bar before placing a fresh napkin in front of the man. He then reaches up for a bottle of Jack Daniels and pours it into a fresh glass with ice, filling it halfway (a little heavy-handed for Jacob's liking) and tops it off with club soda. He spins back around and places the glass in front of his customer. Not another word is spoken. The customer picks up the glass and takes a deep draught, swallowing most of the concoction. He then clunks the glass back down on the bar.

A waitress drops a tray of glasses with a crash, loudly blaming the bartender for overloading her. The lead singer of the band runs some sound system checks as the drummer warms up, and a team of overly-lubricated volleyball players are laughing at the tops of their lungs. None of these distractions draws the attention of Ethan's customer. He is lost in another world.

As a bartender, I never saw myself as a world class chemist. My success stemmed from the rapport I developed with my customers. It doesn't look as though Ethan has mastered that part of the job yet. It isn't just about engaging the jovial bar flies. You have to try and connect with everyone you serve. Old habits die hard, and I feel the need to lend a hand. Picking up my iced tea, I walk down to the other end of the bar.

As I pass Ethan, I wink at him and say, "Watch and learn, newbie."

I ease onto the stool next to the Jack drinker, but he neither looks up nor acknowledges his new neighbor. Not one to be easily deterred, I start the conversation.

"How's it going?" Okay, not exactly engaging, so I'm not surprised that I get no response. "Looks like it's going to be a gorgeous night out there."

Without looking up, the stranger replies, "Did somebody hang a 'Bother Me' sign on my back?"

I look around at the back of his red golf shirt. "Not that I can see."

"Then don't."

"Wow, sorry," I reply. "You looked like you could use a friend."

"Are you a human being? 'Cuz if you are, you're the last creature on Earth I want to communicate with." He picks up the glass for another swallow.

"Looks like somebody pissed in your Corn Flakes this morning," I observe.

"If they had, it would have been the highlight of my day."

"Hey, sorry, man. I didn't come over here to be a pest. I'm not sure what the entire human race did to you, but if you need to vent, I've been told I'm a pretty good listener."

"What's the point?" he murmurs into his glass.

"OK, so no long sentences. How about one word? If you could blame all this unhappiness on one word, what would it be?"

"That's easy. Betrayal," he says, his voice beginning to rise.

"A pretty hot-button word," I say quietly, hoping to keep the conversation calm. "So someone betrayed you?"

"Not someone, everyone. Everyone in my life, they all turned on me."

"What did you do to earn that?"

"That's just it: not a darned thing," he says, turning and looking up at me for the first time. I can see the pain reflected in his eyes. "I tried to be a good husband and father. I was a leader in my church, even started a men's ministry. Our whole social life was built around that community.

"I don't remember when it started to change. My wife began putting the church ahead of me and our children. She withdrew from anything not associated with that congregation."

Tears are starting to water down the Jack Daniels.

"I had to go to church just to be with her. I remember showing up there one afternoon with my daughter, just to say hello. Her car was in the parking lot, but she was nowhere to be found. I walked the halls and asked if anyone had seen her. Everyone seemed nervous, but they all said no. I left without finding her.

"When she came home, she was furious with me. She accused me of following her, checking up on her. I asked her where she had been, and she said she'd had lunch with a friend.

"The following Sunday, when I was ushering at church, the pastor asked to see me after the service. He told me my wife wanted a divorce. I asked him why he was the one telling me instead of my wife. He just stared at me, but I swear I could see the hint of a smile on his face.

"Almost immediately, people at church stopped talking to me. The associate pastor, who had been my best friend from the church, refused to return my calls. It became clear I was no longer welcome at my church."

His pain is washing over me. I am stunned by his tale.

"Do you think your wife and the pastor were involved with each other?"

"I know they were. I found messages on my answering machine to her from him. It was him she was having lunch with that day. But every friend I had in that church deserted me, except one. It was as though 50 of my best friends all died in a plane crash. Other than my kids, I was totally alone in the world.

"And you know what amazes me the most? When I told my divorce attorney the story, he said I had no idea how many times he's heard this same story. Is that what Christianity is all about? A marital merry-go-round? I swear I'll never step foot in a church again as long as I live. When my daughters get married, it had better be on a beach, or I won't be there."

The heat of his anger radiates and burns.

"You know what, man? It's bad enough being abandoned by a church, but I feel like God Himself has totally abandoned me. How unworthy can one man be? Not even God wants to be with me?"

I am the one in agony now. Not only can I feel this man's loss, but I can feel God's, too. How devastating. I take the last sip of my iced tea and look up to find Ethan standing silently in front of me. I push my glass toward him and he clears it away. Ethan reaches for the empty Jack and soda glass, but before he can lift it, I place my hand over the top of the glass and wave him away.

When Ethan delivers a fresh iced tea, he stays close to hear the conversation. I'm not sure he's helping, but I'm not going to make an issue of it. I take another sip and set the glass back down on the bar. Slowly, I turn toward my newest acquaintance.

"First of all, it was rude of me not to introduce myself. My name is David." I reach out my hand hoping for the best.

"Yeah, I'm Michael, but Mike works, too," he says, grasping my hand.

I take a deep breath, hoping for inspiration. My heart tells me to say something to Mike, but my brain can't find the words. Mike and Ethan are both watching me, waiting for a response.

"Look," I start slowly. "I can't begin to know how you feel. I may have walked away from some people in my life, but I was never abandoned the way you have been. I've learned some valuable lessons over the last few weeks; about myself, about life, but mostly about God. I won't debate the fact that you've been deeply hurt. But I might debate where the responsibility lies."

"And who made you an expert? Don't waste your God talk on me. I've heard enough false sermons to last me a lifetime."

"Look Mike, the truth is the church you attended – its leaders and its congregation – were created by man. And man is imperfect. Man built the church, man turned your wife from you, and man turned the people against you. Clearly, that's not the message God intended."

Mike's eyes are locked on mine. My mind is spinning, desperately trying to come up with the right words. I need to be accurate in my guidance.

"The Bible does talk about the church, but in a way that is more synonymous with 'community' than a steepled building. When we pray, Jesus tells us to go into our own private prayer closet and pray alone. He wants us to create a one-to-one relationship with God and pray in a private conversation with just Him."

Mike's body language has changed slightly. He looks up at Ethan and points at his glass. Ethan glances at me quickly and I give him a nod. To my surprise, Ethan already has a drink prepared. Very impressive.

The words coming out of my mouth are not all mine, I realize. It helps to understand that I am being guided through my mission.

I keep going. "Jesus also said not to parade your faith in front of others, that the left hand should not know what the right hand does. Your former church could not tell you that because if that premise were followed, there would be no one to pass the plate. And make no mistake about it, Sunday services are as much about making money for the church and the pastor as they are for your salvation, maybe even more so."

I feel a hand on my shoulder. I look up to see Janice. I smile at her, then turn back to Mike and forge ahead.

"Mike, here's what I have come to believe about my relationship with God. I believe that all the gifts He intends to bestow upon me He gave to me at birth. It's as if there's a small pilot light within me, and He provides me with the ignition. I am blessed with strength, intelligence, integrity, persistence, courage and empathy. I have done some amazing things over the past two weeks, but everything I've done, every characteristic I've exhibited, already existed within me when I started my journey. They are the traits I have always had. But when our path and our gifts intersect, that pilot light ignites a flame within us, burning with a passion that makes us an unstoppable force."

Our conversation has attracted others, and our circle is growing. I can see two more waitresses moving closer and a second bartender has joined Ethan at the bar. Some customers sitting nearby lean in to eavesdrop.

Even Mike seems eager for me to continue, so I push on. "I started out on a journey without any idea how I was going to accomplish the tasks ahead of me. Yet with each step of that journey, every tool I needed in every situation was available to me and always had been. No one sprinkled fairy dust or waved a magic wand over me. I simply responded to those around me with the tools I already possessed.

"The hard truth, Mike, is that you were abandoned by people, not by God. You lost your friends. But if they had really been your friends, they wouldn't have abandoned you. If they truly had Christian hearts, they never would have betrayed you.

"You've had one heck of an obstacle put in your path, one that looks like a mountain. But I have no doubt that you already have the tools you need to scale that mountain. It may be hard to believe right now, but I believe in you. Not because I know you very well, but because I know those gifts are available to you, and I know that

God could not possibly desert you. He equipped you. He equipped you because He loves you, not because He can't stand to be in your company. The real answers are not in the bottom of that glass. The answers lie within you, Mike. God gave you the answers when you were created. The rest is up to you."

Mike starts to speak then clears his throat. "So you're saying I shouldn't blame others for what I'm going through?"

"I'm saying that when you blame others, you give them control over your life. I'm saying focus on controlling the things you can control. If you give others control over your emotions you give them power over you. Keep that power and take back control of who you are.

"Let me tell you a parable of sorts. You are in a small boat in the upper Niagara River, a short distance above Niagara Falls. The engine dies and you're drifting toward the rapids and a trip over the Falls. As I see it, you have two options. You can drop to your knees and pray to God to save you. Or you can dig out the oar and paddle like hell for shore. One way you're hoping for a miracle, the other has you drawing on your own strength, determination and intelligence that you're given at birth, your gifts. The first turns power over to hope. The second keeps power in your hands. Which option would you choose?"

Mike doesn't look up. He's embarrassed by the tears streaming down his face. He's trying to catch his breath between sobs.

"I've lost so much, but I'm so tired of feeling this way, tired of my kids seeing me so weak. And no matter how many bottles of Jack that I go through, it never removes the memories." The tears continue.

"Mike, the memories won't go away. The video will keep playing and you can't change it. But you can change the audio. Play a different tape. Tell yourself that what you have gone through has brought you closer to your children. Good things have come out of all of this pain. Play that tape!" I stand up and move closer to him, placing my hand on his shoulder. He finally looks up, rises and gives me a hug. Janice's hand is still on my shoulder, and Ethan is smiling broadly. The response of those around us catches my attention. Smiles seem to be contagious, heads are nodding and more than a few hugs are shared.

As I look at those who have gathered to hear us talk, I find a pair of familiar eyes staring back at me. Much to my surprise, Jacob is standing at the back of the group. I push through the crowd and we embrace as long lost friends.

"How long have you been standing here?" I ask.

"Probably from pretty close to the beginning," replied Jacob. "Listen, my young friend, with all your e-mails, your sisters' Facebook narrative, and what I heard here tonight, you don't belong in a club. It doesn't feel right anymore. You have too much to offer the world to be stuck behind a bar."

I look back at him, slightly puzzled. "What are you saying?"

"What I'm saying is that there's no longer a place for you here. It appears you've found your true calling. You need to devote your energy to that. It doesn't mean I won't miss the hell out of you or won't continue to insist on e-mails, but there are people out there who need you much more than I do."

We embrace again, patting each other on the back. I turn back to Mike, who is now shaking hands with those who had gathered around him. Our eyes meet. He smiles and nods. The glass of Jack in front of him remains untouched.

I lean across the bar and shake Ethan's hand. "It's all yours now," I tell him. "And by the way, it's always Jacob, never Jake."

Ethan smiles back at me. "I got it. Thanks. But I think I'm a long way from doing what you just did."

"Six months ago, I would have thought the same thing. Let me tell you something, Ethan. Jacob is as great a boss as you will ever find in your life. If you like the bar business, stay close to him, learn from him. He is the best and he will make you the best. You seem like a smart, talented kid. Most kids your age have no work ethic. Develop that, and anything you want from this life will be yours." With that, I turn toward the double doors. Cheers are still coming from the volleyball courts, but the band nearly drowns them out. I look back one last time to find Jacob's eyes following me across the deck. I know how difficult it must have been for Jacob to send me packing. But he's always been a good and decent man – and apparently more perceptive than I've given him credit for being.

I turn the corner, heading to my Jeep, invisible to the partying crowd around me. Yet I am surrounded by warmth and by eyes that follow and protect my every step.

My path is now my home.

19

The Prodigal Son

It is just after 9:00 when I pull the Jeep back on the road. The sun is just setting over Lake Erie. The wispy summer clouds are tinged a deeper shade of orange with each passing mile. I leave the beachside roads and continue north along Route 5, through Hamburg and into Lackawanna. I pass through the ghost town of Bethlehem Steel, a victim of the dying rust belt. The Jeep shoots up onto the Skyway, which overlooks a waterfront that is finally starting to evolve into the gem all of Western New York thought it could be. As the elevated highway peaks, construction lights illuminate the Arena to my right and the headlights of vehicles backed up on the Peace Bridge shimmer over the international waters to my left. The bright red tail lights on the bridge mark the end of another day of shopping for our Canadian neighbors; white headlights announce the end of another day on the beach for Buffalonians.

I am less than 20 minutes from home now, and my concentration is divided. I can't wait to see my family, but I can't stop thinking about what had just happened at the Breakwall. I think back to the embrace I shared with Mike and the phenomenon of changing another life. I don't know if these changes are permanent, but I feel that Mike has enough to work on and think about to help find hope in the days ahead.

Things could not have ended any better with Jacob. I had no idea how I was going to tell him I wasn't coming back, but he took care of that himself.

The Jeep is practically on autopilot now, traveling down familiar streets. It always feels strange to return to the old neighborhood. Everything seems smaller, shrunken. My memories of these streets from my childhood are so big. Coming back as an adult throws off my perspective.

I have no idea if anyone will be home, but it doesn't feel right to announce my return in advance. Just slipping in might give me the best chance of having some quiet time with my family. It is almost 10:00 when I turn into the driveway and park in my old spot. Lights are on inside and out, but the family car is not in its place. I grab my backpack and walk through the garage into the kitchen.

Jeannie and Hannah are sitting at the kitchen table, each with a laptop in front of her, laughing at the images on their screens. I let my backpack drop loudly to the floor, and they whip their heads around. Both jump up and come running, Hannah letting out a squeal as she rushes into my arms.

She quickly pulls away and grabs my arm. "Come here, you gotta see this." She pulls me like a dog on a leash over to the table.

While I was traveling, Jeannie had created a Facebook page in my honor, dubbing it "The Flockless Shepherd." It started as a gathering place for family and friends, but Jacob quickly started sharing it with friends and followers and linked it to the Facebook pages of each of his clubs. In a matter of days, the page went viral. Within two weeks, more than 400,000 people had liked the page and were regular followers. All of my e-mails appear there in their entirety. There are e-mails from some of the people I had encountered along the way, telling their stories of how we met. A link to a newspaper article in the Beckley, West Virginia News is a prominent recent addition.

Kevin had written a song about his accident and the man who reunited him with his father. Terry posted a drawing of himself in an Oberlin sweatshirt and me mussing his father's hair. It was actually pretty good. People were claiming to have met me in places I never visited. Even Jacob had written a testimonial to the best friend he had ever had.

Suddenly, Jeannie jumps up.

"Oh my God! I almost forgot something!" She grabs her cell phone and runs out of the room.

"What was all that about?" I ask Hannah. She just smiles and shrugs.

I sit at the kitchen table and continue to be amazed at what I see on the screen. I had no idea I had become so famous. Those who are following the webpage call themselves "The Flock." I am touched beyond words. Hannah puts her arms around me and tells me how proud everyone is of me.

"I'm the most famous girl in school," she says.

"You mean guys are actually asking you out?" Hannah punches me in the arm.

"In fact they are," she announces proudly.

"So does that mean I don't have to take out the garbage anymore?" That earns me another punch. Just then Jeannie bounces back into the room, throwing her phone back on the table.

"What is up with you?" I ask.

"Nothing," is the only response I get, so I let it go.

We spend some time scrolling through the Flockless Shepherd page. The girls keep stopping me to show me their favorite comments. Whatever hardships I had endured during the journey, this makes it all worthwhile. I have never felt closer to my sisters than I do right now. Their joy knows no bounds. They are laughing and giggling nonstop, competing to see who can get closer to me and monopolize more of my attention. I was used to Hannah behaving like this, but even Jeannie is lost in the moment. Best of all is the pride they have in their brother. As siblings, we haven't always gotten along, but this is exactly what I craved in our relationship. I flash back to when I didn't think Jeannie would ever forgive me for disappearing to Nashville. It wasn't that long ago that I thought we might never recover from the pain I had caused both of them.

Just then, the door from the garage flies open and Mom and Dad come running into the kitchen.

"Davey!" Mom screams, and buries me in an embrace. Dad is not far behind. He wraps his massive arms around both of us. More than a few tears are shed. Not a word is spoken. Even the girls, watching from a distance, join in the crying. Never has this family shared a moment like this.

Even as the group hug ends, Mom can't take her hand from my sleeve. Dad suggests we move into the family room so everyone can hear about my adventures. I fill them in on what has transpired since my last e-mail, and have their undivided attention. Mom is the only one who leaves the room, but only to return with glasses of lemonade for everyone.

When I reach the end of the story about Mike and Jacob, it's well past midnight, and Mom and Dad suggest it's time for the girls to head to bed. After some mild resistance, they give in. I get one last hug from each and then they both trek up to their rooms. Mom decides it is her bedtime, too, so she leaves the room to father and son.

This is the moment I have looked forward to often since I left home, but never more so than during the final leg of the trip, especially after parting ways with Eamon. I have so much I want to say to my father, but now that the time has come, I am tongue-tied. We both sit in silence.

After what feels like a month, I finally break the ice. "Dad, I have so much I want to thank you for. I don't think this trip would have happened were it not for you."

"Why do you say that?" Dad asks.

"Because it was you who painted the vision of a path in life. It stuck in my head all these years. You told me God had a path for me, and that someday, I would find it. But before anyone else could believe in me, I had to believe in myself first. That's why my trip to Nashville failed. You planted that seed, and I had to know I was following the lead of something far greater than me – and not just music. It also meant a lot that you trusted me to make the right decisions. You never tried to talk me out of working for Jacob or leaving him for some strange pilgrimage."

"David, I've always had faith in you. And I've always had faith in God. I knew that somehow those two beliefs would find each other. While I felt you were destined for great things, I had no idea you would have such influence over the people in your life. I am so very proud of you and so thankful that you came home so I could tell you that, and tell you how much I love you."

My eyes are brimming once again. I had always respected Dad, but we'd seemed to be at odds so much of the time.

"Dad, I can't even find the words right now to tell you how much I love you and how much I appreciate the foundation you've provided me. I spent so much time being angry with you for finding God and leaving me behind. Part of me was jealous. I know now that I was so wrong not to trust you. I know I have never told you this, but you truly are my hero. Always have been, always will be."

He reaches over and pats my forearm. This time he breaks the silence. "So, tell me son, where do you go from here? What's next?"

"You know, I've learned to not even try to predict what tomorrow will bring. I feel at peace when I am helping others. Nothing in my life has ever felt so right. But I don't know if I'll be doing it forever. I can tell you I learned a great deal about myself. I came to know the real me, and I like what I've found. It's like I told Mike, I have gifts inside me that I never knew I had. I haven't become someone new as a result of my accident, I've simply found the real me that survived that deathbed. The messenger who visited me didn't give me new skills or talents. He just gave me a chance to use the ones already inside me. As for where all this takes me, I don't know, Dad, I really don't."

"I don't know either, David. But what I do know is that I believe in you. Whatever you decide, I don't doubt it will be the right thing. As I've always said, once you find that path, don't stray. You may never find your way back to it again."

I rise from the couch and give Dad one last hug. "I'm heading to bed, Dad. It's been a very long couple of days." I grab my backpack and throw it over my shoulder as I head for the stairs. As my foot hits the first step, the doorbell rings.

Dad rises from his chair. "Who in the world could that be at this hour?"

I look up and see Jeannie and Hannah at the top of the stairs watching me. Jeannie points to the door. Something is definitely going on.

"Dad, relax. I think I'm supposed to get it," I call back into the family room. I set my pack on the step and walk through the foyer. I flick the porch light on and see a familiar figure on the steps. I open the door.

"Peg!"

"Hi, Davey."

"What are you doing here? How did you know? Oh, wait a minute. Did you get a call from Jeannie tonight?" She offers a sheepish grin. "Well, that explains that," I smile.

"I asked her to call me if you came back. Don't blame her."

"It's okay. But why are you here?" I repeat.

"Because I want to talk to you. You know, during our entire time together, I never just showed up at your house; I always waited to be invited. But this is important. Do you have time?"

"Sure, Peg." I step out on the porch and pull the door closed behind me. We sit down on the steps.

She is clearly nervous. She turns to face me. "Davey, it's been more than two years since you left for Nashville. I was so mad at you. I couldn't believe you were walking away from what we had. I decided to move on and not look back. I dated for a while, but to be honest, you never left my heart. I was so scared to come here tonight, scared of how you might react. But I saw the real you in the Facebook page your family made for you. I'm so proud of you, of all you've done. You're the man I fell in love with, believed in. I just wanted to tell you that. And to let you know that I miss you, more than I ever thought possible. I've fought this for so long, tried forcing my heart in other directions, but it's always come back to you."

She is shaking, and a single tear is making its way slowly down her cheek. She throws her arms around my neck and holds on tight.

I hold her close. This is the moment I have dreamed of so many times, albeit a little different than I'd imagined it. I'd never forgotten how she felt in my arms, the gentleness of her touch, that Peg smell that I loved and that drove me crazy. Without even thinking, I pull my head back and kiss her. It feels so familiar, like we had kissed only yesterday. Then I hold her close, wishing it could last forever.

I slide my hands down her arms and gently push us apart. Our eyes lock. "First of all, Peg, for what it's worth, I never stopped loving you either, not for a heartbeat. And there's never been another woman since you, not even a kiss. Whether you believe it or not, Nashville was for both of us, for both of our dreams."

"I know that Davey. I just didn't believe you'd ever come back to me."

"Peg, not a day has gone by that I haven't thought about you. These last two weeks on the road, I wished you were right there with me. But I discovered myself on that road and I don't know what I'm supposed to do now. I'm not sure my journey is over. I have so much to think about, and our talk tonight has added a whole new dimension to my thoughts. I'm more confused now than before."

"I kinda thought you'd say that, Davey. I can't make those decisions for you. You have to do what you feel as right. It's just that I have come to a realization. I can't imagine spending my life without you. I couldn't always say that before. I am so proud of who you have become and so proud to have you in my heart."

"Peg, how about this. Whether I decide to go or not, let's build this slowly. We have been apart for almost two years. Both of us have been through a lot. We can talk every day, see each other whenever we can, be sure this is what we want. We don't have to make any decisions tonight. We know we love each other. I believe that what we have is strong enough to survive the path I have to follow and the decisions I have to make."

"Davey, if you need to keep going, go. I will be here for you whenever you need me. Maybe there will come a time when we walk your path together. Either way, my heart is yours and always will be. I will leave the next step up to you. You decide. This is why I came here tonight. To let you know I'll always be here for you."

"The miracles of this day just keep coming." We hug again and kiss one last time before she turns and walks down the driveway. I watch her go and keep watching until the taillights disappear.

I walk back into the house, which is mostly dark now. My bag is still at the bottom of the stairs. I walk slowly up and back to my old bedroom. I set the bag on the floor just inside the door and, without turning on the light, climb straight into bed. It's nearly 3:00. My head hits the pillow, but my eyes aren't ready to close yet. Dad's final words weigh heavily on my heart. *"Once you find your path, don't stray from it. You may never find your way back."* This is the deep thought that ends a very long day.

"So tell me, son, where do you go from here?" The words of a father to a son. Yes, where do I go from here? How do I stay on the path? So many lives touched, so many more to go.

"Don't stray, for you may never find your way back again."

Then sleep finally overwhelms me, even though there is still so much to decide and so many options to choose from.

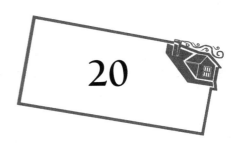

20

The Awakening

MY EYES OPEN SLOWLY. THE sun is shining on the wall next to my bed, the windows are open and a soft breeze causes the curtains to dance. I sit up and look around my room. My backpack has been emptied and is by the desk. My clothes are cleaned and folded and sitting on the chair next to my desk. How did Mom manage to do this – get the laundry done without a sound and still get to work on time?

The house is unnaturally quiet. Everyone must be following their daily routine. I cross to the bathroom and take advantage of the privacy and a full tank of hot water, intending to indulge in a long, leisurely shower. Dad had spent years maximizing the water pressure until it was like a daily massage. This shower has always been my favorite place to think.

Despite being alone and with nothing planned for the day, I feel hurried. Once out of the shower, I dress quickly. I take a full inventory of my room, logging the memories of each item. From the posters on the wall to the trophies on the shelf, to the pictures spread over my desk, this room has been my diving board. When I left for college, I'd stood in this same spot preparing to leave home for the first time. When I decided to go to Nashville, this was where I made that final decision. It was in this room where I told Peggy that I loved her for the very first time. When I left to start my journey, packing my bag on this bed was the last thing I did before heading out.

Now, here I am again, knowing it is time to launch myself one more time. I turn toward the bed and lean my knees into the mattress. I reach down and pick a shirt off the top of the pile. It was the one I was wearing when I dove into the Chesapeake Bay to find Ange. As I stare at the shirt, thinking of the grizzled soldier, I look up and see the sunlight on the wall grow brighter. At first, I think the wind has separated the curtains, allowing the sun to shine directly into the room. But then I realize it is brighter than just the morning sun. I turn slowly to see a familiar form behind me.

"Hello again, young shepherd." It is my messenger, standing in the doorway of my bedroom. His white robe shines brightly, filling the room with light. His hands are clasped before him and his eyes stare intently into mine.

"You have done well, David."

"Thank you," I squeak as my voice fails me.

"The Father has sent me to deliver a message. You made a promise to Him to serve if your life was saved. You honored that promise and served very well. The Father is pleased with you. I am here to tell you that you have been released from your commitment. You have paid your debt and are now free to live your life in any way you choose. You should know that many have made a promise such as yours, but none have done as well and few have ever been released from such a bond."

"I don't know what to say."

"There is nothing you need to say. Do you have a message with which I should return?'

Without hesitation, I say, "Yes, there is one request I would like to make."

"As long as you know I have no authority to respond to what you ask. I will carry your request back for you."

"My request is simple. I ask not to be released, that I be allowed to continue to serve as I have done the last few weeks."

The messenger pauses, and with a pensive gaze replies, "Now I am the one surprised. May I ask why?"

"I appreciate the gifts I have been given. And I have never been as fulfilled as in His service. I feel I have much more to give. I don't believe you can put a value on a life. Mine was saved so that I might serve, and serving is the best thing I've ever done. So, with all due respect, I would like to continue packing my bag and be your Father's tool wherever I am needed."

The messenger appears satisfied with my answer.

"First, you should know that He is not just my Father, He is yours as well. Secondly, I don't believe I need to take that message back," he replies. "No one who asks to serve is ever denied that opportunity."

Just then, I hear a noise coming from the window. I glance outside but see nothing. When I look back, the messenger is gone. In his place, leaning against the doorframe, is a long walking stick with a large hook at the top. A shepherd's staff.

All I can do is smile. So much looks the same, yet everything has changed. Dad and I are back where we belong. Mom is happy. The girls were never closer and their brother is once again their hero. Jacob is content with our friendship and Peggy and I are in love and ready to build a future together.

With everything in place, my path beckons. I refill the backpack, sling it over my shoulder and look around the room one more time. I have no doubt now that it is time to go. My path is clear and is laid out before me. Not the one running through the field to the public pool. Not the one guarded by my beloved oak tree where Dougie saved my life. But one that draws my heart to serve the One who seeks lost sheep to bring them home.

I am honored to serve. I am honored to have been found and saved. Honored, too, to have a flock that will discover the value of lifting each other up and, in doing so, discover their own gifts.

What more can a shepherd ask for his flock?

The Beginning

About the Author

A LIFE LONG WESTERN NEW Yorker, Gary Friedman has a Bachelor's degree in management/marketing and a Master's degree in counselor/education, both from Canisius College in Buffalo. His three vastly different careers encompassing 17 years in retail management, eight years in education, and the past twenty years working for the federal government, have exposed him to a wide variety of people from all walks of life. With the completion of his first novel, he has fulfilled a goal from the very top of his bucket list. Like his shepherd, he has always sought to lift up those around him and touch their lives in a positive way.